THE CREATURE IN THE CABIN

A SOUL SEEKER COZY MYSTERY #3

COURTNEY MCFARLIN

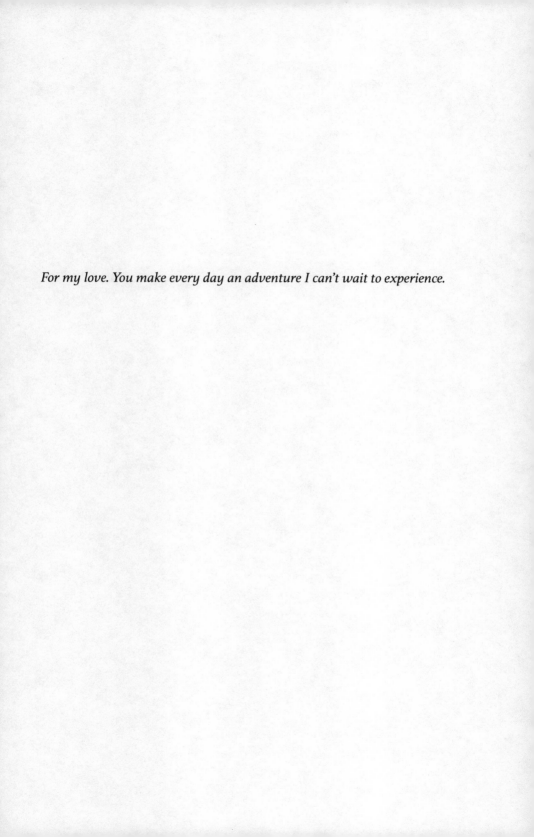

For my love. You make every day an adventure I can't wait to experience.

1

As I made my way up the winding road to the top of the mountain, I resisted looking to my right. I'm not much for heights, and the drop-off just past the guardrail was at least a thousand feet. Okay, it was like three-hundred. Still, it was a super long way down. A long, bumpy way down filled with sharp rocks.

At least there was a guardrail, I told myself as I focused on the road ahead of me. Traffic was light, but there were a few mining vehicles lumbering up the pass, and I didn't want to come around the corner and smack into one. I rolled the windows down so I could inhale the fresh, pine scented air. Something about that smell always grounded me and cleared my head.

I'd grown up in the small town of Gilded City, South Dakota, and was more than happy to still call it home. The infamous city of Deadwood was just down the mountain and it was filled with historic properties that made my job as an interior designer and home stager a genuine pleasure.

I rounded another sharp curve and headed up the last stretch of road, grateful it was still summer and the roads were clear. This mountain resort was not a place you wanted to get caught in during rainy or snowy weather, even if you had good tires. Luxury cabins came into view and I let out a whistle as I saw one that had been recently built. Its front was completely covered in windows and I would put money on it having a million dollar view from the inside. Most of the cabins operated as short-term rentals, and they were usually hard to get, even when it wasn't ski season.

I turned down a dirt road and a beautiful cabin came into view. Unlike its surrounding neighbors, this property looked more like an old mining camp, rather than a modern vision of luxury. I appreciated the attention to detail, from the rustic siding to the metal roof that was artfully designed to make it look rusty, while remaining watertight. I came to a stop next to a huge SUV and took a deep breath. Here we go.

A tall woman was pacing back and forth on the porch as I got out of my vehicle and headed in her direction. She was on the phone, talking in a rapid-fire voice that I recognized from her call the day before. I waved and hung way back as she continued pacing, her high heels making sharp rapping sounds on the wood decking. She held up a finger towards me and kept talking.

I turned around and looked out over the property, appreciating the simple beauty of the place. The lot was lined with trees and it had an amazing view down to the valley below. I squinted and could just make out the shape of the hills that surrounded the city of Creekside, way below.

"Sorry about that," she said as she ended her call. "I'm Liz Freed. Are you Brynn Sullivan?"

"Yes, we spoke yesterday. You mentioned some odd things were happening here?" I asked, noticing she looked indecisive. "It's okay. You can trust me. Whatever you say will be held in strict confidence. I understand it's difficult to talk about spiritual things."

I knew this all too well. While my company, Sullivan Staging, paid my bills, my life's work was assisting ghosts and other supernatural beings. For whatever reason, I'd been able to see and talk to ghosts from a very young age and I'd helped many of them move over to the other side. It was only recently that I'd truly embraced who I really was and what I could do, and I still found it difficult to bring up in normal conversation.

She huffed a laugh and motioned for me to follow her inside.

"You're very tactful. Bob Tremaine said you were the perfect person to call and I can see why. Yes, we've had several strange reports from our renters and they're leaving critical reviews. This market is so competitive we won't be able to keep renting it out if this keeps happening. New cabins are getting built every day and while this place has been popular, our star average is dropping every day. At this rate, we won't even be able to give free nights away to get people to rent it."

We stepped into the foyer of the cabin and I looked around in awe at the interior. It was full of beautiful wood trim and accents, and the design combined luxurious fabrics and finishes, while keeping the rustic vibe intact. This was a gorgeous property. I couldn't resist running my hand over the wooden banister on the stairs as we stood there.

"Can you share what people have been saying?"

She delicately chewed on her thumb nail before frowning and removing her hand, giving her head a slight shake.

"I don't understand it. All the reports have said that they've seen a strange, bear-like creature. It's been spotted here, in the house, and just outside, by the deck. I'm not from here. I work out of Rapid Falls, but I'm pretty sure there aren't any bears in the hills."

"I sure hope not. I know we have the occasional mountain lion, but bear reports are pretty rare. And I certainly have heard nothing about bears in homes."

"Well, I don't know what it is, and I don't care. I just want it gone. Our group will pay whatever you want if you'll help us out. Bob said you were the person for the job and highly recommended you."

"It's not about the money," I said as I walked around the living room. "Do you have a record of all the reviews?"

"Unfortunately, they're all out there in the open. If you put in the address for the property in any of the rental sites, you'll be able to find them."

"I see. Do you mind if I look around?"

She glanced at her watch before looking back at me.

"I need to run. Would you mind locking the place up? If you're interested in taking on this, um, project, send me a text and I'll shoot you over a contract. We'll want you to sign an NDA before you start."

"Sure, that will be fine. I shouldn't be too long. I'll text you when I leave."

She gave me a brisk nod and swiveled in place, heading for the door in rapid strides. The sound of her heels on the polished wood floor echoed as she left. I took a moment to settle as I walked into the kitchen, wishing I'd brought my cat, Bernie, with me. I'd owned the beautiful black cat ever since I was a little girl, and he was an amazing partner for communicating with ghosts. Usually, he wanted to tag along when I went on a job, but today, he'd been nowhere to be found. Apparently, he had important cat business that I wasn't privy to.

I walked back towards the staircase and listened, straining my ears for any hint of movement or odd sounds. Ghosts were typically quite shy, and it was strange this one, if that's what it was, was so active. I gulped before heading up the stairs. At least I hoped it was a ghost and not an actual bear.

The upstairs loft had beautiful tongue-and-groove wood paneling on the walls that matched the wood on the ceiling. I headed into the bathroom and hesitantly looked into the mirror, remembering my recent encounter with a banshee in a local hotel. I was still finishing up my interior design work on that project, but luckily, I'd helped the banshee move on after she'd been trapped in that place for decades.

The bathroom was empty and there wasn't an icy chill that usually accompanied ghostly visitors. I shrugged and headed back down the stairs, taking a seat on the last step. The place was quiet, and there wasn't a sign that something spiritual was going on. After waiting for a few minutes, I remembered Liz said some people saw the creature out on the back deck, so I headed in that direction.

The view from the sliding glass doors that opened onto the deck was breathtaking. The pines swayed gently in the breeze and the blue sky winked through their boughs as they twisted back and forth.

I pulled out one of the deck chairs and sat, drinking in the scenery and enjoying the feeling of quiet peace. This was certainly an odd case. How could a place that felt this serene be involved in so many reports of a disturbance?

Well, if the spirit wouldn't come to me, maybe I could go to it. I got up and walked down the steps of the deck into the yard below. The grass was soft underneath my tennis shoes as I headed towards the trees. The light faded as I walked into the forest, and the soft sound of wind whispering was peaceful. I rubbed my arms, wishing I'd brought a hoodie, as I walked through the trees. Even though it was a toasty eighty some degrees down in town, it was a brisk sixty up here.

Something rustled ahead of me on the trail I was following. I paused and tried to look around the trees to see what it was. It was most likely a deer. At least, I sure hoped it was. While it was incredibly rare to sight a bear in these woods, I supposed it could happen. I stopped and looked around as the rustling sound increased to a crashing noise. Uh oh, this wasn't good.

I backpedaled and felt the hair on the back of my neck raise as the temperature dipped even further. Oh dear, what had I gotten myself into? Memories of the banshee's scream and pointed teeth flashed through my mind, urging me to walk faster. While it had all turned out in the end, my first encounter with the banshee was something I would never forget. I wasn't in any hurry to repeat that experience.

The crashing sounds grew louder, and I chanced a look over my shoulder. The tree limbs were moving violently just down the trail. Whatever it was, it looked like it was huge. This was not a dear. Okay, enough was enough. Time to get out of here and get to safety inside the cabin. I walked faster, forcing myself not to run. If it was a bear, the last thing I wanted to do was run, right? Or should I drop into a fetal position? My mind raced faster than my feet as I made it out of the trees and hit the grass behind the cabin.

I jogged up the steps and looked back over my shoulder. A loud crack of a breaking branch made me jump. I could see something dark emerge from the trees and my breath caught in my chest. It was misshapen and my brain couldn't quite compute what I was seeing. I resisted the urge to step closer to get a better look and slowly backed towards the sliding doors, reaching out for them with a hand while keeping my eyes on the creature.

It shuffled closer, making strange noises, and I whimpered as I fumbled with the handle behind me. I finally got it open and darted inside, closing the door as fast as I could.

The creature stopped, and it looked like it was scenting the air. I searched for what I thought was its face, looking for eyes, but I couldn't make anything out. It let out a fearsome howl that I could hear through the glass doors before it vanished.

My heart skipped another beat, and I felt a cold sweat break out over my body. I rushed through the house and ran to my vehicle, feeling secure once I was safely inside. I locked the doors and turned the key, determined to get the heck out of this situation. I didn't know what that was, and I wasn't sure I wanted to.

2

I made it halfway down the mountain when it occurred to me I hadn't checked to make sure the doors were locked. I cursed softly to myself and looked for a place to turn around. As much as I didn't want to go back up there, I didn't want to leave the place unlocked, either. I was in the middle of beating myself up about it when my phone rang. My lips quirked into a smile as soon as I saw the name on the screen.

"Hey, how's my favorite girl?" Zane asked.

Zane Matthews was a newly transplanted security expert who'd left New York for our small town. He was way more handsome than any man had a right to be, and he was also my boyfriend. We'd met a few short weeks ago and while it hadn't been smooth sailing the entire time, I was falling for this guy pretty fast. We'd gone on our first official date the night before, and the memory of his soft kisses made me lose track of my thoughts. What was I doing again? Oh right, answering him.

"Well," I said, stalling for time as I tried to figure out how to respond to his question. "This place up here is pretty interesting."

"What's going on?"

I found a scenic pull-out and turned in so I could head back up the mountain. Having Zane on the other end of the phone made me feel safer as I motored back to the cursed cabin. I told him what I'd seen and I could hear the tension in his voice.

"Brynn, I don't want you going back up there if it isn't safe. Dear God, a bear could eat you in seconds. What are you thinking?"

"That's the thing. I'm pretty sure it's not an actual bear. Besides, it literally disappeared. Like, poof. I think we're dealing with something else entirely."

"Pretty sure isn't doing much for me right now. I can be up there in twenty minutes if you'll wait for me."

"That's sweet of you, Zane, but I think it's okay. I'll just lock the doors really quick and head back down. We can talk about our date last night while I drive."

"Nice try, but that won't distract me. Are there bears in the Black Hills?"

"Well, it sure distracted me there for a few minutes," I said, grinning as I drove down the dirt road back to the cabin.

He chuckled softly before answering.

"It was pretty amazing. You still haven't answered my question about bears."

"Careful, your city is showing. We might have one bear sighted every five years. Give or take a year. There are a few over the border in Wyoming, and occasionally they widen their territory and end up here. Typically, they're taken down to that bear sanctuary in the southern hills."

"Occasionally and typically aren't doing anything to lower my blood pressure."

"It will be fine. I'm 95% sure it wasn't a bear. If it was, it's a brand new kind that can wink out of existence. I'm here, I'm going to walk up to the door."

I took a deep breath as I darted out of the car and jogged to the front door. Nope, I hadn't locked it. At least this trip hadn't been in vain. I went back to the sliding doors, made sure they were locked, and then headed back outside, checking the lock twice just to be on the safe side.

"Brynn, do you see anything?"

"Nope, it's all clear. I'm getting back in my vehicle."

He let out a gigantic sigh, and I backed down the driveway. I couldn't believe that just the day before, I'd gotten myself into a crazy situation with a whacko who worked in the hotel where the banshee was found. He'd kept me hostage, but thanks to the help of some friendly ghosts, the banshee and my wonder cat Bernie, I'd gotten free and he'd been arrested.

"You get into the strangest situations," Zane said finally.

The grin slipped off my face as I thought about what he could mean, and I didn't answer him right away. Was it all too much for him? When he'd first found out I could talk to ghosts, he'd freaked out temporarily, but eventually he'd come around. He'd been present yesterday when I'd helped the banshee, Molly McElhone, cross over to the other side. While he had seen nothing, he'd definitely felt it. Would he be okay with this side of my business picking up?

"Hey, Brynn. Are you still there?"

"Yeah, sorry. Just lost in thought."

"It's not like a bad thing, just a new thing. For me, anyway. I'll adapt," Zane said, seeming to sense my hesitation.

I couldn't shake the worry that hung around in the back of my head, even as I processed what he was saying. I'd avoided relationships like the plague and I wasn't used to putting myself out there. Throughout school I'd been known as the weird ghost girl and it had taken me years and the help of my cousin, Logan, to get through it all. Dating hadn't been in the picture. I tried to shake off my inner self-doubt.

"So, anyway, I need to decide if this job is something I want to take on. They want me to sign an NDA. I need to do some research before I get back to Liz."

"Want any help with that? I'd be happy to come over tonight if you'd like some company. I'll even cook."

"Wait, you cook?"

He chuckled again, and the warm, deep sound made my stomach flutter.

"Baby, I grew up in an Italian neighborhood. You don't even know the skills I have."

My eyebrow hiked up to my forehead, and I blushed as I thought about what he could mean. We hadn't taken our relationship beyond kissing, and it was way too soon to think about it. Focus, Brynn.

"Alright, well, let's see what you can do," I said, trying to sound braver than I felt. "I love Italian food."

"Sounds good to me. I'll be done with work here in an hour and I'll go do some shopping. See you at your place in two hours?"

"I'll be there."

I ended the call and tried to get my jumbled thoughts in a row. First things first. I needed to figure out what that creature was. Typically, the ghosts I dealt with were of the human variety. Was there such a thing as a bear ghost? I didn't think so, but I guess there's a first time for everything. I'd never dealt with a banshee until a few days ago, so I definitely had a lot to learn about the spirit world.

I checked the clock on my dash and saw that I had just enough time to stop by the county clerk's office and pull the records for the property. Maybe I could learn something from them. I turned onto the highway and set the cruise control as I turned up the radio. If I couldn't figure out what I needed to know there, I could always visit my friend Sophie at the library tomorrow. She loved helping me with my cases.

Within a few minutes, I found a place to park at the county building and walked inside. It was another scorching day, and I appreciated the cool wave of air conditioned air as it wafted over me.

Luckily, the clerk's office was empty when I walked in and I spotted my friend Janice looking bored as she leaned against the counter.

"Brynn! It's great to see you. What can I help you with?"

"Hi, Janice. I've got another property for you to pull."

"Ooo, where's this one?"

I rattled off the address, and she typed it into her computer, gazing at her screen. I resisted the urge to lean across the counter to peek at the results when she let out a little gasp.

"That sounds interesting."

"This is old. These are always the best to look up. Hang on, I'll get it printed out."

Janice was another history buff, and she always liked to help me with my cases. She may not have been a firm believer in ghosts, but she loved learning more about the properties I worked on. The printer kept spitting out pages, and I raised my eyebrow.

"Wow, there must be a lot of detail."

The Victorian house I'd recently worked on had a huge file, and from the amount of paper shooting out of her high-speed printer, this one looked like it was going to be even bigger. It must date back even further than I thought.

"It looks like it's on the site of an old mining claim," she said as she started organizing the sheets.

The printer finally quit, and she put the last few sheets on the bottom. I grabbed my wallet to pay the fee.

"Have any exciting plans for the weekend, Janice?"

"Same old, same old. Trying to beat the heat. We may head out on the trails though and do a little hiking. Winter will be here before you know it. How about you?"

I eased the giant stack of papers into my tote, glad I had just enough room to fit it all. This was going to be some serious reading. I nodded at my bag.

"You're looking at it. I can't wait to dig into this one."

"Let me know if you find anything interesting."

"Will do. See you later. Thanks for your help."

I headed back to my car, looking around downtown as I walked. Deadwood was a happening place, and as usual, tourists were everywhere. They were the lifeblood of our little area, and the city management did a great job of making sure there was an event nearly every weekend. From the looks of it, there was another big festival planned. I'd have to check to see if it was something Zane would want to check out. I still had plenty of time to make it home, so I pulled into the Diamond Deb hotel parking lot.

My cousin, Logan, was still working on a huge remodeling project on the fourth floor, and there were a few things I needed to button up on my part of the project. Our fathers had sold him their construction company when my dad retired and moved to Arizona and Logan was doing an amazing job growing the business.

I walked through the lobby and punched the button on the elevator, feeling a chill run through me as I waited. So much had happened since yesterday morning when I'd gone up to work on the design phase of the remodel. The doors slid open, and I hit the button for the fourth floor, grateful I wasn't going back down into the basement. That was one area of the hotel I planned to avoid for the rest of my life if I could. I had more than enough of it the day before.

The doors slid open and I could hear the sounds of Logan's crew, working hard on turning the existing rooms into luxury suites. I headed in the noise's direction and leaned against the doorway, waiting for Logan to finish what he was working on. His handsome face brightened when spotted me and he nodded to one of his workers before joining me in the hall.

"Copper Top! How's my favorite cousin? What are you up to?"

"Still your only cousin. I wanted to see if there was anything else I needed to finish up here before I head home for the day. Did Kelsie get a crew up here to remove the cameras?"

He grimaced, and I made a face, still creeped out by what the former hotel employee had done. We'd discovered his network of hidden cameras he'd installed in the rooms, and that he'd been murdering guests. If it hadn't been for my friends, I might have been added to his list.

"Yeah, they got rid of those this morning. I guess there were way more than they thought. Kels said her bosses were furious and scrambling to make sure word doesn't get out about it."

Kelsie Thomas was the manager of the hotel, and she'd gone to high school with us. While she'd been one of the mean girls back then, we'd both matured and we were working towards being friends. Logan might have been working on being a little more than friends with her, something I couldn't wait to tease him about. Logan had played the field for years, but I had a feeling that was about to change.

"I can only imagine how bad that would be for the hotel's reputation. How long is it going to take you to get these suites ready for phase two?" I asked, giving him an elbow in the ribs.

We may have been cousins, but we were just five months apart and he felt more like a brother to me. He stuck out his tongue at me. Yeah, we're not very mature. That's just how we roll.

"Ouch, you have the pointiest elbows. Now that we don't have to worry about creepy screaming happening every few minutes and freaking my guys out, we should be able to get all the framing finished by next week. I finally have a full crew."

I smiled to myself, remembering the peace I'd seen on Molly McElhone's face before she made it to the other side. What I'd seen reflected there was going to stay with me for the rest of my life. She'd been through unimaginable pain before she'd died, and it had turned her from a regular ghost into a tormented banshee. She'd been warning people of their imminent deaths by appearing in the mirror of Room 413 and screaming. It had been the most unearthly sound, but now she was finally at peace.

"Well, while I'm waiting for you to finish, I can start on this new project, I guess."

Logan waggled his eyebrows and leaned closer.

"Is this about the cabin? What did you find?"

I launched into the story of what I'd seen on the mountain and his face grew serious as he listened.

"It's most likely not a bear, but I honestly don't know what it could be," I said, finishing my story.

Logan knew all about my abilities and had protected me from the worst of the teasing throughout our time in school. While he may not have been able to see what I could see, he was always there for me.

"That sounds crazy dangerous, Brynn. Haven't you had enough excitement lately? I know I have."

"No kidding. But if this is someone who needs help, I can't just walk away. I'll dig into the cabin's history tonight and see what I can learn."

"Just be careful. Do you have a hot date planned for Zane tonight? I suppose you won't have time for your poor cousin, now."

He winked at me, and I rolled my eyes.

"As if. Besides, I'm going to guess you're taking Kelsie out tonight, anyway."

He gave his boyish grin that was notorious for melting hearts, and I shook my head.

"Maybe. Call me later if you find anything interesting."

"Laters. Get back to work."

I nudged him again, chuckling as he rubbed at his side.

"Geez, you should have a license for those things. See you later, Brynn."

I went back to the elevator, pushed the button for the lobby, and stepped in. As the doors opened back up into the lobby, I spotted Kelsie at the front desk, but she was busy helping someone check in, so I gave her a wave and headed back outside. Her pretty face brightened with a smile and she waved back.

I hoped she might be the one that would convince Logan to settle down, something I never thought I would have said just a week ago. How things change. I got back in my car and headed down the highway. I'd have just enough time to get ready before Zane showed up. A little zip of excitement went through my core as I drove.

3

As soon as I swung open my front door, Bernie ran towards me at a jog, meowing the entire way. I scooped him up and gave him a big hug, stroking his black fur as he purred at me. I set him down and he headed straight for the kitchen, where he turned and looked at me expectantly.

"Alright, alright. I'm coming. Let me put down this heavy bag."

I swung my tote containing the file on the cabin onto my kitchen table and joined Bernie in the kitchen. I sorted through the cans, looking for a flavor I knew he'd appreciate. I remembered how he'd specifically asked for chicken when we were both in what he liked to call the in-between. Wherever that was. But the coolest thing was we could communicate with each other when we were there.

I dished up his food and looked down into his beautiful green eyes, wishing we could talk all the time.

"Bern, do you ever wish we could talk to each other?"

He gave a noncommittal meow and bumped me hard on the leg.

"Okay, okay, more food, less talk. I get it."

I slid his dish in front of him and walked back to the bedroom, debating on what to wear for tonight's dinner. It had been a long day and the last thing I felt like doing was getting dressed up. A shower though? Yeah, that was needed. Stress sweat is real. What can I say? And I'd been plenty stressed out earlier.

I hopped in the shower and lathered up my hair, thinking about what I'd seen earlier. It couldn't have been a bear, but what was it? It certainly hadn't appeared human, that was for sure. I finished up my routine and walked back into the bedroom. Bernie was waiting on the bed, curled in a ball.

"Hey, bud. I know you picked out my outfit last night. How about a little help tonight? Zane's coming over to cook."

He cracked an eye, gave me the kitty equivalent of a shrug, and went back to sleep. Okay then, I guess I was on my own. I pulled out a fresh pair of yoga pants and a tee shirt. I don't know why I stressed out on getting dressed up for Zane when he saw me practically every day wearing a pair of jeans and a tee. Tonight, I was going for comfort. I combed through my tangled, wet hair and scrunched up the waves, debating on whether to put on makeup. I shrugged and made a face at myself in the mirror.

A knock on the door interrupted my indecision, and I jogged through the hallway to open it. Zane had what looked to be half the contents of the grocery story hanging in plastic bags off his arms, and I hurried to help him.

"Oh my goodness, why didn't you let me know you needed help?" I asked, grabbing two bags off his arm.

He struggled towards the kitchen and levered the bags up on the counter. Men.

"Two trips are for weaklings," he said, giving me a wink.

His icy blue eyes made me weak in the knees, and have I mentioned yet that he smelled fantastic? Well, he did. His longish, black hair was brushed off his face, and he was wearing my favorite pair of faded blue jeans and a vintage tee. Yum.

"Still, I would've been happy to help. Are you feeding an army, tonight?" I asked, adding my two bags to the collection on the counter.

"I wasn't sure what you had for staples, and I got a little carried away."

I cocked my head to the side and tried to keep from grinning.

"Staples? Like the metal thingies for paper?"

He let out a laugh and pulled me in for a hug.

"You're adorable. I mean like spices, noodles, stuff you keep in your pantry. That kind of thing."

"Just kidding. I know what they are. It probably was a good idea to get some of those. I'm afraid my culinary prowess includes heating soup and making grilled cheese sandwiches."

"Well, now you'll be able to branch out a little. Add some oregano to your soup or something."

I shrugged and started emptying the bags, sorting through everything he'd purchased. I let out a squeal when I saw the fresh baguette sticking out of the last bag.

"Are we having garlic bread?"

"We are indeed. I have a complete meal planned for you. All you need to do is sit there and tell me more about your day."

"At least let me help with something."

He looked around at the pile of food and back at me, apparently trying to figure out what wouldn't be too much of a challenge for my non-cooking skills.

"The salad. You can get that ready while we talk."

"Sounds good."

I searched through my cupboards until I found my big popcorn bowl, figuring it could hold something a little healthier than its usual contents of butter and salt, as I re-created my afternoon for Zane. He was chopping something that smelled divine while the water boiled. I couldn't resist peeking over his shoulder. Since he was so tall and I wasn't, it was more challenging than it sounded.

"Whatcha doing there?"

"Trade secret. Want to cut up some tomatoes for the salad?"

"Fine, give me the busy work."

I grinned at him as I got to work dicing the tomatoes. Bernie sauntered in and stretched out, lifting each leg and spreading his little toe beans apart. I was just about to comment on the beauty of those same toe beans when he shot me a look. I shrugged and got back to work as he jumped up to monitor my work. From the expression on his little kitty face, I couldn't tell if I was doing it right, but I soldiered on.

"How was your day?" I asked. "All we've done is talk about me."

"It was interesting. I got a new client in Creekside who reported they've had some strange thefts in their store."

"Really? What's going on?"

"They can't explain it. Apparently, some time during the night, a few items have been disappearing. I'm guessing it's an employee with access, but we won't know until I get the cameras installed."

"Huh, that sounds strange. Anything else for me to do? That smells amazing," I said, leaning over the counter to get a view of the bubbling pots.

"That's it. Tell me more about this cabin. What are the reviews saying?"

"Good idea. I haven't looked those up yet. I'll grab my laptop."

I slid my laptop out of my tote bag and set it up on the counter while he worked. I perched on the bar stool and waited for the browser to load before searching

for one of the more popular vacation sites in the area. Once I added in the address, the cabin popped right up. I could see the rating was at three stars and I figured that wasn't a good thing.

"What are you seeing?" Zane asked, looking at me over his shoulder while he stirred what I assumed was sauce.

"Well, the overall rating is a three. That's not good, right? I haven't used one of these sites before."

He grimaced and nodded.

"Yeah, that's veering into the don't stay here at any price territory."

"Let's see what some reviews say."

I started at the beginning and it looked like until a few months ago, everyone had only glowing things to say about the cabin. The reviews were a mix of four and five stars, and there was no mention of anything bad. I re-sorted the list so I could see the most recent reviews and my eyebrows raised.

"That doesn't look good," Zane said, watching my face.

"It's not. This most recent one was from last week. They

mentioned seeing the same thing I did, coupled with a noxious odor that wouldn't leave the cabin. They gave it a one-star. Well, at least whatever it was didn't let out a stink when I was there."

I went back to reading through the newest reviews and they all mentioned similar issues. A few of them brought up strange noises and cold pockets, a definite indicator that something spiritual was going on. I closed the laptop and put it back in my bag before taking an appreciative sniff of the air.

"I know that smells good though, whatever it is you're making."

Zane grinned at me, his eyes crinkling in the corners.

"I hope you enjoy it. This is one of my favorite recipes. The garlic bread is about done."

I clapped my hands and scooted around the counter so I could help. I grabbed an oven mitt and took the pan out of the oven, breathing in the garlicky goodness.

"Oh, wow. I could just eat this and be completely happy. This smells way better than store-bought."

He rinsed the pasta, and I grabbed some plates from the cupboards, trying to sneak a peek into the other pot as I did.

"Hey, no peeking. I'll get this plated up and bring it over to the table if you want to slice the bread and grab the salad."

I mock-pouted a little as I followed his directions and got everything set up at the table. Bernie thumped down from his spot and took up his usual begging position at the end of the table.

"Bernie! You probably shouldn't sit on the table when we have company."

"He's fine," Zane said, delivering my plate with a flourish. "For my sweetheart."

My eyes widened as I saw the concoction in front of me.

"This is amazing. What is it?"

"Pasta Carbonara. I hope you like it."

He looked uncharacteristically unsure of himself, and I rushed to smile at him, wanting to put him at ease.

"If it tastes half as good as it smells, it will probably be the best thing I've ever had."

He chuckled, and we both dug into our plates. I'd like to say I was very ladylike and polite, taking only dainty bites, but I'd be lying. I shoveled that pasta in as fast as I could get it on my fork and cleared my plate before I knew what happened. Zane gave me a delighted grin.

"You like it?"

"Oh my, I love it. You need to make this like every night. I'm not even kidding. I've barely touched my salad."

"That makes me so happy. My neighbor, Mrs. Fratelli, taught me how to make this when I was a teenager. She said the best way to the heart of the future love of my life would be this dish. It looks like she was right."

I blushed a little as his words sank in, not believing my luck. A handsome man who was built like a superhero and could make pasta like this? Sign me up for a lifetime subscription, please.

Bernie let out a piteous little mew that made us laugh. Zane picked up a piece of noodle and offered it to my cat, pausing and giving me a quick look.

"He can eat this, right? There's no sauce on it."

I nodded, not wanting to reply around my enormous mouthful of garlic bread. Bernie licked the noodle tentatively before swallowing the whole thing whole. I guess he takes after me.

We made quick work of the rest of our meal and I sat back, still savoring the flavors. Zane moved to take the plates away, and I jumped up to stop him.

"When you make a meal like that, I do the dishes," I said, taking his plate and stacking it on mine.

"I'll at least keep you company. Do you think you're going to take on this new project?"

I rinsed the dishes off in the sink before loading them into the dishwasher as I thought about his question. I was too intrigued to walk away. I'd seen nothing like that, and I wanted to figure it out. I nodded as I finished loading the last dish.

"I think I will. I pulled the report on the property from the county and I'll go through that later and see what I can learn. There's got to be an explanation."

"And you're sure it's not a bear?" Zane asked, crinkling his brow.

"I'm positive. Bears don't act like that. At least I'm pretty sure they don't. No, it's something else entirely."

I walked around the counter and took Zane by the hand, leading him into the living room.

"Want to watch a movie?"

He wrapped an arm around my waist and we sank down onto the couch. Bernie hopped up next to Zane and purred while he got settled.

"What would you like to see?" Zane asked.

"Anything. Let's see what's on the DVR."

As Zane was scrolling through the listings of what I'd recorded, my phone rang. I let out a groan, not wanting to move from my comfy spot. I couldn't ignore the ringing, though. I heaved myself up, promising myself I'd go for a jog or at least a walk tomorrow to work off all that pasta, and grabbed my phone from the table.

"Sullivan Staging."

"Brynn, it's Liz Freed. Have you decided if this project is something you can help us with?"

I thought for a second, knowing I wouldn't be able to take back my decision once it was made. I glanced over at the couch and met Bernie's green gaze. He nodded. Good enough for me.

"Yes, I'll help. Please send over that contract and I'll get started right away."

"I'm not familiar with how this will all, um, work," Liz said, sounding hesitant.

"I'm going to do some research on the property. In the meantime, I might need to access the cabin at different times of the day. Do you have anyone renting it during the next week?"

"Yes, actually. We have a big party booked for tomorrow through the weekend. After that, I can block it off for as long as you need it. I'd cancel this booking, but the owner is adamant that this is all just a smear campaign against his property. He doesn't want to lose money with cancellations. He's agreed to give us a week with no reservations to figure it out. I'm actually going out of town after this group checks in, but you'll be able to reach me by phone."

"I see. Well, I guess I'll do what I can dig up and wait to go back up there. If anything odd happens, or this group reports any problems, please let me know. I can be up there within a few minutes."

"Thanks, Brynn. I never thought I'd be in this position, but I'm really glad Bob introduced us. I'll email over the agreements for you and the code you'll need to access the property."

"I'll get them signed and sent back."

She ended the call, and I glanced back at the couch. I couldn't turn back now. While it would've been nice to get back to the cabin tomorrow, I could do my research in the meantime. I walked back to the couch and couldn't help but smile at the sight of Bernie curled up in Zane's lap. I snuggled into his side and closed my eyes, savoring the moment. The strange occurrences at the cabin could wait until tomorrow. Tonight, I was going to enjoy chilling on the couch, watching a movie with my cat, and my boyfriend. A happy flush worked its way across my cheeks as Zane wrapped his arm around me and pulled me closer.

4

T he morning sun peeked through my curtains, waking me way earlier than I normally get up. I rolled over in bed and found Bernie, flat on his back, all four feet in the air, sleeping soundly. I rubbed his tummy, risking the needle claws I was sure would be wrapped around my wrist in mere seconds. He gave a little chirp and looked at me sweetly for a beat before doing just that.

"Ouch! I never learn, do I?" I asked him, moving my hand to the safer territory of his head.

He stretched and gave me a look that summed up his feelings on the matter eloquently. I ruffled his fur and stretched out next to him, looking up at the patterns the light was making on the ceiling as I thought about the night before. Zane and I had watched a movie before he headed home, giving me another one of his patented kisses that made my toes curl. I hugged my arms around my chest and smiled to myself before rolling out of bed.

I headed to the kitchen to get my coffee brewing, eyeing the tote bag that was still sitting on the kitchen table. That reminded me I needed to check my email and see if Liz had sent over the documents she wanted me to sign. I filled my mug and pulled up my email account on my phone. Yep, she'd sent them. Luckily, they were all in digital format, so a few clicks later, I'd signed the NDA and agreed to their terms, which were more than fair.

Bernie wandered into the kitchen and sat at my feet, yawning hugely before giving a little chirp.

"I suppose it's not too early for your breakfast, is it?"

I got his food ready and thought about whether I wanted anything to eat, but the enormous meal I'd eaten the night before meant I wasn't even close to being hungry. I grabbed another cup of coffee and went over to the table, ready to dig into the history of the cabin. I checked the time before I started reading. I still had two hours before the library opened, which gave me plenty of time to get through this gigantic stack of papers.

The property abstract was mind-numbingly boring, which was typical, but I noticed that a new owner, Trent Mason, had taken possession of the place a few months ago. I made a note to check to see if that timing coincided with when the critical reviews started. If I hadn't seen the creature myself, I'd be tempted to think what Liz said about the owner was correct, that he felt someone was trying to ruin him. I went back to the file and kept reading.

Janice was right. The property itself sat on an old mining claim that was registered back in 1874, right at the start of the gold rush in the Black Hills. The state had still been a territory back in those times, and the law was set by whoever had the most power. Deadwood was a crazy place back then, but I loved the fact you could live shoulder to shoulder with so much history, even if some of it wasn't the nicest.

I kept reading but learned little beyond the fact that the current cabin had been built on the site of an old miner's shack. I shivered, remembering I had little luck with old shacks. Bernie jumped on the table and started pawing through the papers, an intent look on his face. I let him, knowing he had an uncanny ability to ferret out information that I might have missed. He punctured a sheet with one of his claws and looked over at me.

I gently disengaged his claw and read over what he'd found. Interesting. It looked like the original claim, filed by Edward Davis, had been disputed in 1877, right as the old gold rush petered out. Herbert Mason was awarded the claim. I couldn't help but wonder if the current owner was a descendent of Herbert, or if that was just a strange coincidence. I put both sheets together, wishing I had a stapler handy. I grabbed my notebook and made a list of the names of everyone who had owned the property to date. I glanced over at Bernie, who was sitting on the table, chest puffed out, looking very important.

"Thank you, Bernie. That could be significant."

He gave me a majestic nod before hopping down from the table and strolling to the front door before sitting in front of his carrier. I looked at the time on my phone.

"I guess it is time to head to the library, isn't it? Are you going to come with me today?"

He sat in his kennel and kneaded at the soft, plush lining impatiently.

"Fine, fine, I'm coming. Let me get dressed and grab another cup of coffee first."

He sank down with a sigh, placing his head between his paws. I hustled back to the bedroom to change. Yes, I totally let my cat boss me around. What can I say? I'm a sucker.

A few minutes later, I'd loaded a thoroughly impatient and cranky Bernie into my car and drove to the library. I couldn't wait to see what my good friend, Sophie Ryman, had to say about this latest case. She'd been such a big part of my life, she was an honorary aunt. I loved her Bohemian style and open mind, and knew a lot about who I was becoming as an adult was because of her amazing influence.

It was still a little chilly, so I rolled the windows down a little and parked in the shade.

"Ready, bud? I don't think Sophie will mind if I bring you in, but you'll need to stay in your bag, okay?"

He gave a soft meow, which I took to be his grudging acceptance of the rules. I walked up the sidewalk, admiring the architecture of the library for probably the thousandth time. The Greek revival pillars shone softly in the morning sun and I took a deep breath of the mountain air as I walked inside.

A librarian I didn't recognize was manning the front desk, so I shifted Bernie's bag so it was slightly behind me. I didn't know how she'd react to seeing I'd brought my cat with me. She gave me a friendly smile and a nod as I approached.

"Hi, is Sophie in today?" I asked.

"Coming, darling," Sophie said from the office to the left of the desk.

I heard her bracelets jingling before I saw her. She was dressed in one of her many flowing skirts, topped with a brilliant purple tunic. I couldn't help but grin as she enveloped me in a hug.

"Have you met Stacia? She's our newest recruit. Today is her first day."

"Hi, Stacia," I said. "I guess it's a little early to ask if you like working here since you just started."

"Oh, I love books and this place is like heaven on earth," she said in a quiet voice. "I've dreamt of this throughout school."

"You're a natural, dear," Sophie said, chucking her under the chin. "Now, what brings you in here today, Brynn? You can't possibly have a fresh case yet, the last one is hardly cold."

I glanced over her shoulder at Stacia, and Sophie took the hint.

"Come, my dear, to the Dakota room. I'm sure whatever you're working on can be answered there."

I followed Sophie as she swept towards my favorite room in the library. It held hundreds of books and archives on Deadwood's colorful past, and she was right. It usually held the answers I needed.

She shut the door behind us and looked at me expectantly.

"Sophie, you'll never believe what I saw yesterday. Sorry, I didn't know if I wanted to include Stacia in this discussion."

"No worries, dear. Now, tell me everything."

I sat down in a chair at the long table and put Bernie's carrier down. She smiled at him and unzipped the door slightly so she could stroke his head.

"I'm sorry I can't let you out, you magnificent cat. I'm afraid the library has strict rules for animals. Although, maybe you are a service animal, in a way."

Bernie stretched up and butted her hand and purred loudly before settling down again as if to let her know he understood, even if he didn't agree.

I laid out what I'd seen the day before and what I'd learned this morning. Sophie listened raptly, tucking her salt-and-pepper hair behind an ear absentmindedly.

"I see. First a banshee, and now this. What on earth could this creature be? I know, let me find a book on local legends."

She sprang to her feet, and I shook my head, hoping that when I reached her age, I'd have half the energy she did. I glanced over at Bernie, and he blinked slowly at me.

Sophie came bustling back with her arms full and plopped down next to me, shoving a book in my direction.

"Wow, I didn't expect you'd find so many books," I said, cracking open the cover gently.

"This place is full of interesting finds," she said, opening a book of her own. "You never know what you'll learn. Sometimes I take my lunch breaks here and choose a book at random. In fact, I think I might have read something before that will come in handy, today. I just need to find it again."

We were both quiet as we read. I paged through my book, treating the old pages with reverence as I looked for anything that might be relevant. Most of the legends seemed to surround unsettled ghosts. I wondered if any of them were still around. One of these days, if things ever slowed down, I'd have to go on a ghost hunt to see if there were any that needed help.

Sophie gave a loud cry, and I jumped in my seat, startled.

"What did you find?"

She slid the book over to me, marking a spot on the page with a long, elegant finger.

"I think this might be pertinent, dear."

I started reading and nodded my head. The passage talked about a strange creature that had been spotted on that mountain back in the late 1890s. The language was old and stilted, but it mentioned a bear-like creature being spotted. I turned to look at Sophie, excitement racing through my veins.

"This is exactly like what I saw! I wish there were other accounts."

"We'll just have to keep looking."

"Do you have any logs of the old mining claims from that area?"

"I can find them. Keep reading and I'll be right back."

She jumped again and disappeared into the stacks. I read through the book she'd handed me, but found nothing else that seemed to fit what I'd seen. She came back holding another stack of books.

"Here we are, a list of all the mining claims from the mid-1870s. They're organized by name, so I hope you already pulled the abstract for that cabin."

I fished my notebook out of my bag and held it up triumphantly.

"I did. The first claim was filed by Edward Davis in 1874."

She went through the index and excitedly flipped to the middle of the book.

"Found him! He held the claim for three years, and then it was transferred in 1877 to a Herbert Mason. Let me find him."

After peeking at the index, she turned to the right page and let out a low whistle.

"Herbert Mason owned a lot of claims. It looks like he was quite the mover and shaker back in those times. Look at this, dear."

The list of claims registered under his name was long. Bernie gave a loud meow from his bag, startling me. He was staring through the mesh with an intensity I'd rarely seen out of him. I needed to find out more about these men.

"Sophie, do you mind if I go to the newspaper archive? I want to see what I can learn about Edward and Herbert. It might not be related, but something tells me I might find at least some answers there."

"Of course. I need to go check on Stacia, but please look up whatever you need. I'll be in to help in a little while."

"I'll put these away first. Do you mind if I check out the book on the legends, though? I'd like to read the whole thing."

"Of course, I'll put it on your tab."

I stacked the books she'd given me and quickly sorted them onto the right shelves before slipping the book I wanted to keep into my bag. I grabbed Bernie's carrier and headed for the newspaper room, excited to have some concrete leads.

Not all the old papers had been digitized yet, but the old microfiche machine was still in working order. The first local paper had published in 1876, so I knew I wouldn't find much information before that date. I flipped to the beginning of the paper and tried not to get distracted by the other stories as I read, looking for a mention of Edward or Herbert. So much had happened during the first few years of Deadwood's founding, and the paper was full of unique ads and funny stories.

By the time I reached the edition published back in September 1877, I finally found the first entry related to both men. A brief story was published detailing their feud. It looked like Herbert owned a nearby claim and said that his original boundary included the area claimed by Edward. They'd argued over it for years. I assumed the feud only got worse when the local mining board finally decided in Herbert's favor. Quite a lot of gold had been extracted by that point, and they ruled Edward had to turn over all of his proceeds.

I sat back and glanced at Bernie.

"Wow, that would've been a blow to old Edward. All of that hard work and he had to give all the money away. Crazy."

I kept reading, finally finding a notice of Edward's death in 1878. There was a brief obituary which stated he'd died of unknown causes up in the hills. The actual date of his death was unknown, but his decayed body had been found by a hunter in the fall. Interesting. I wondered how'd he met his end and if this was all somehow related to what was going on at the cabin now. It seemed like a stretch, but I had little to go on. I glanced through a few more years, noticing that Herbert Mason was indeed a powerful man, even if he wasn't well liked.

He died in 1921, leaving a son behind. There was no mention of a wife or any other relatives. I made a few notes and reset the machine.

What to do now? It wasn't quite lunch time, yet. I called Liz and see when the group who'd booked the cabin was going to check-in. Maybe I could take Bernie up to the cabin with me.

I dialed her number, and she answered on the third ring, sounding as if she was stressed.

"Brynn, thanks for sending over those documents. Did you need anything?"

"Actually, I was wondering when that group you mentioned was going to be at the cabin? I'd like to go back up there if I could."

"Perfect timing. If you go up there now, the cleaning woman should still be there and she can let you in. I need to get you a copy of the code so you can come and go once this group checks out. They shouldn't be there until after three this afternoon, so you should have plenty of time."

"Great, I'll head up that way, now."

"If they leave before you, don't forget to lock up."

"I will, thanks," I said, ending the call and turning to Bernie. "Ready to go see if we can find the creature?"

He let out a loud meow, and I chuckled as I grabbed the straps of his bag. I'll take that as a resounding yes. I waved to Sophie and Stacia as I left, not wanting to bother them in the middle of their training session. Sophie gave me a wink and held up her hand in the universal 'call me' gesture. I nodded and headed out into the warm sunshine. Time to go back up the mountain.

5

The trip back up the mountain wasn't as harrowing thanks to Bernie's company. It was a gorgeous summer day and traffic was light as we headed to the cabin. I looked over at Bernie, who was sitting in the passenger seat, gazing across the hills with a faraway look in his eyes.

"Bernie, do you ever want to go out and enjoy the wilderness? I could get you a harness and you could be an adventure cat."

He glanced over at me and narrowed his eyes.

"Or not. Whichever."

He gave a sigh and turned away, and I'm pretty sure he shook his head as if to let me know how silly my question was. Cats.

I pulled up into the driveway of the cabin and loaded Bernie back into his carrier. There was another car parked in the drive and the front door of the house was open. As I walked up to the stairs, I could hear loud music playing.

"Hello? Is anyone here?" I asked, looking around the living room.

"Gah! You scared the stuffing out of me," a woman said as I rounded the corner into the kitchen.

She had red hair that was even redder than mine, a feat I hadn't thought possible. Her long tunic was stained with dust and she looked like she'd been working hard.

"I'm so sorry. I'm Brynn Sullivan. I talked with Liz and she said I could come on up before the next group checked in."

I really didn't want to let her know why I was there, but maybe she knew something. Bernie gave a soft meow from his bag.

"Is that a cat?" she asked, blinking at me like I was from another planet.

"Yeah, this is Bernie. He often comes with me on my jobs."

"You're not a new cleaning lady, are you? I just got this gig, and I thought they liked my work."

Her shoulders tensed, and I rushed to put her at ease.

"No, not at all. The place looks lovely. I've been hired as a consultant for the, um, cabin rental agency."

Smooth Brynn, real smooth. I was never good when I was on the spot. I smiled when I saw her shoulders relax and she gave me a much friendlier look.

"I'm Susanna. I run my own business. A consultant, huh?"

"Something like that. I won't be a bother. I'm just going to look around, if that's okay?"

"Suit yourself. I'm almost done here," she said, eying Bernie's bag. "I've already vacuumed."

"He won't shed, I promise."

"Likely story. Cats are all shedding machines. It's a good thing they're so darn cute."

"If he does, I'll clean it myself."

She looked at me closely and nodded, apparently satisfied.

"All right, then. If you need anything, I should be around for another ten minutes."

"Thanks. Susanna, you said you've cleaned up here before. Have you ever noticed anything, I don't know, odd?"

She gave me another close look and snorted.

"Lady, I clean rental cabins for a living. I see odd stuff every day. You're gonna have to be a little more specific."

I put Bernie's bag on the floor and went for it. If she thought I was crazy, I guess there wasn't much I could do about it.

"I mean, have you ever seen or experienced anything that isn't, well, human?"

She let out a booming laugh that startled me.

"Some things I run into might be classified as that. I clean the whole place, sheets included, if you know what I mean."

Oh, gross. I really didn't need that mental image in my head right now. I let it go, figuring I needed to focus on why I was there.

"I see. Well, I'll let you get back to work."

I headed up the stairs with Bernie's bag, but paused when she spoke again.

"Wait. There is one thing, but I don't know."

"Yes?"

"Well, I guess you could say that lately, there's been a strange feeling in here. Like I'm not alone. I probably sound crazy, but that's how I'd describe it."

"Have you ever heard anything?"

She narrowed her eyes at me.

"You one of them ghost hunters, like I see on television?"

I was debating on how to answer that when Bernie gave a loud meow. Okay, cat, I guess I'll put myself out there.

"Something like that."

"Hmph. I don't know about all of that stuff, but it is fun to watch. Sometimes, the hair on the back of my neck stands up. You know what I mean? I just go about my tasks. If the place is haunted, that's none of my business. As long as they leave me alone, I leave them alone."

"Thanks, Susanna. I appreciate it."

She turned back to her cleaning, and I headed up the stairs. Once Bernie was free, I started with the bedrooms, walking around slowly, trying to get a feel for anything odd. Bernie scooted under the bed and I whispered to him.

"Try not to shed."

He gave an annoyed meow and disappeared under the bed frame. I guess that told me. I walked into the next bedroom and looked out the window, into the forest, remembering what I'd seen the day before. Everything was quiet now. I hadn't imagined the whole thing, had I?

I shook my head and continued exploring the bedrooms. Nothing. I walked back into the hall and noticed a hatch that must lead to the attic. The string to pull down the stairs was just out of reach. Did I dare go up there? Bernie meowed softly at my feet, staring at the string.

"Really? I don't know about this."

He gave me a long look and then returned his attention to the string. Either he wanted to play a rousing game of catch the string or he wanted me to go up into the attic. Somehow, I figured he wasn't in a playful mood. Great, just great. I searched the rooms until I found a chair I could move into the hall. I stood on it and pulled the string, releasing the stairs. They let out a loud creaking noise, and I looked around, hoping Susanna hadn't noticed. She shouted from the bottom of the stairs. Dang it.

"What are you doing up there?"

"Just going up into the attic. Sorry about all the noise."

"As long as you clean up any dust that falls. I'm not redoing my work."

"I will."

I looked up the stairs, wondering how sturdy they were. As I was thinking about how much I really didn't want to go up there, Bernie shot past me and took the stairs two at a time. Really? I swallowed the lump in my throat and followed him, determined that I would not get shown up by my cat. The attic was dark, and from what I could make out, not that clean. I pulled my phone out of my pocket and hit the flashlight app, turning around so I could see what I was getting into.

"Bernie?"

I looked around, searching for his eyes. There! I walked in his direction, gingerly stepping as the old boards creaked under my weight. I did not want to end up crashing through the floor, especially considering how much pasta I'd inhaled the night before.

I came to a stop where I'd last seen Bernie's eyes, but he was long gone, investigating some corner I couldn't access. I turned in a circle, shining my light. All I could see was old furniture that had been piled up. I heard Bernie's meow from my left and shuffled in that direction.

"Buddy, where are you?"

He gave a little chirp, and I about fell over him as I came to a stop in front of a wooden chest. I knelt in front of it, excited by his find.

"This looks promising. I wonder what's inside?"

I tried to open the lid, but it wouldn't budge. I moved my light around the sides and found an old padlock that looked rusted shut. Darn it.

"Sorry, Bern. I have nothing to open it."

He started pawing at the side and I shook my head.

"We'll have to come back with some tools. I bet there's something really interesting in there."

"Brynn, or whatever your name is? I'm leaving. Make sure you lock the place up."

I went to the hatch in the attic floor and looked down to see Susanna standing there.

"You wouldn't have a screwdriver or a hammer, would you?"

She snorted and shook her head.

"Not on me. I don't think they keep any tools here, either. Anyway, I'm leaving. See you around."

Okay, that wasn't helpful. Bernie scampered past me and I paused at the top of the rickety stairs to take one last look. The hair on my arms stood up, and I held up my light. What felt like a breeze wafted past my head and I shivered, looking around for the source. I stepped back from the stairs and peered into the darkness. Suddenly, a rush of air came at me, making me step back. I teetered at the top of the stairs before finding my balance. Yeah, that wasn't helping my fear of heights any. I decided enough was enough and slowly backed down the stairs, holding on tight with one hand as I held my phone up.

"Get out, get out, get out," said a raspy voice.

"Who's there?"

Bernie let out an ear-splitting screech, and I glanced down to see that he was puffed up to about twice his size. He made the same sound again, and I stuffed the phone in my pocket so I could move faster.

I chanced one more look up the stairs once I was on solid ground. Bernie stalked back and forth and let out a hiss, displaying his fangs and looking for the world like a mini, irate panther.

I yanked on the string to send the stairs back up, letting go as I felt it tug on my arm. It slammed shut with a bang. A cold sweat broke out over my forehead as I strained my ears, wondering if I'd hear the voice again.

Everything went silent for a second, minus the soft sounds of Bernie padding back and forth.

"What do you think, Bernie?"

He glanced over his shoulder at me and kept walking back and forth, scenting the air and curling up his lip. I looked at him strangely until the smell smacked me right in the face. Oh dear heaven, what was that odor?

It had to be one of the most rancid smells I'd ever encountered. All I could think of as I hustled Bernie into his bag and headed back downstairs was that it was a good thing Susanna left, or she might have thought I was the source of the terrible stink. I gagged once I reached the bottom of the stairs and looked back over my shoulder.

"Get out."

There was that voice again, and it sounded like it was right in my ear. I jumped and hurried to the door. This time, I made sure the lock was engaged and slammed the door behind me. I knew it probably wouldn't keep whatever was in there from following me, but it sure felt good.

I got back in my car and unzipped Bernie's bag. He shook himself thoroughly before bathing his coat with rapid strokes. I took a tentative sniff, hoping the stink hadn't joined us on our mad dash out of the cabin. Whew, we were in the clear.

I stared at the cabin for a few minutes, wracking my brain to figure out what was going on. If only I could talk to Bernie right now, like I could when we were in the in-between. It would be so much easier. I said as much to him and he paused mid-lick before giving me a soft meow. I guess he felt the same way. I sighed as I started the car and backed down the drive. More research was definitely going to be needed. I headed for home, determined to dig into the phenomenon and figure out what the heck was going on.

6

Once we were safely home, I grabbed the book Sophie had given me and sat down at the table to read. I briefly wished the book had an index so I could look up anything with a strange stink, but unfortunately, I came up empty. I started at the beginning and kept my notebook handy in case I found something that might be pertinent.

As I read, I came across the entry I'd found earlier about the bear-like creature. I made a note that it was first seen around what was now the ski resort back in 1891. From that point on, the book noted it appeared on and off, before finally disappearing after 1895. I kept reading, but couldn't find anything else that seemed related.

I sat there, stumped, trying to find the connection. The creature was spotted before the turn of the century, and then disappeared, or at least wasn't spotted until just a few months ago. There had to be a connection between the inciting events.

"What do you think, Bernie? Are they related?"

He jumped on the table and pawed at my bag. I slid out my notes from earlier and remembered the new owner shared the same last name as Herbert Mason, the man who'd feuded with Edward Davis.

"Thanks. You're as helpful as Lassie," I said, ruffling up the fur on Bernie's head.

His eyes narrowed until all that was visible was a slight gleam of angry emerald green. Whoops.

"Um, I mean you're incredibly brilliant and there's no dog on earth who could compare to your majesty."

He flicked his tail at me before jumping down. I guess I was on my own. Since the appearances started right after he purchased the place, I needed to see what happened during the 1890s when the bear creature was first reported. I grabbed the file folder with the property abstract and started reading. It looked like Herbert Mason was given the deed to the claim in 1877. I needed to learn more about the mine. I turned back to my laptop and went through the remaining results from my search on Mason. I finally found an entry that looked promising and clicked on the link.

"Listen to this, Bernie. It looks like the claim Mason got from Davis didn't amount to anything until the spring of 1891, when he discovered a vein that paid out big time. He'd got around three hundred thousand dollars out of it before it went dry. I wonder how much that would be in today's dollars?"

I heard a loud meow from the bedroom, which I took to mean I'd interrupted his nap and shrugged. I pulled up a conversion app and let out a gasp. That was the equivalent of over seven million dollars today. Wow.

So, the mine had paid out, and the creature appeared. Once the mine went dry a few years later, it disappeared. There just had to be a connection between the creature and Edward Davis.

The light outside faded, and I realized I was sitting in near darkness, lit only by the screen of my computer. I flipped on the lights and shuffled to the kitchen, wishing I had some leftovers of that amazing pasta Zane had made. I opened the fridge and stared inside, wishing food would materialize. I shut the door and opened it again, just in case. Nope, still nothing.

My phone rang, and I smiled when I saw Zane's name on the screen.

"Hey, master chef. How's it going?"

He let out a laugh, but I could tell he was tired from the strain in his voice. ˙

"Good, it's been a long day and I'm not done yet."

"What's up?"

"That client we talked about last night. We finally came to an agreement on his security system and he wants it installed tonight while no one is there. He's convinced it's an employee, and he wants to catch them in the act."

"You've got to work all night?"

"Looks like it. I wanted to take you out to dinner tonight, too. I'm sorry Brynn."

"Hey, it's okay. Maybe we can have lunch tomorrow instead?"

"My treat. How did your day go?"

"I went back up to the cabin after my visit to the library."

I could feel him tense through the phone.

"Why didn't you tell me? I would have gone as back-up for you."

"That's sweet, but you said it yourself. You were tied up with work all day. I'm still researching what's going on up there, but I think it's safe to say we're dealing with something spiritual."

"What happened?"

"Nothing big. Besides, the sooner you get back to installing that system, the sooner you'll be done. I'll tell you about it at lunch."

He let out a sigh and I could picture him tucking his hair behind his ear.

"Sounds good. I want a full report."

"Yes, sir."

Zane chuckled before signing off.

"Good night, Brynn. See you tomorrow."

"Later, Matthews."

"Later, Sullivan."

I ended the call and hollered for Bernie.

"Bernie, what do you want for supper?"

Apparently, that was enough enticement to get him to come out of the bedroom. I heard four little feet hit the floor and come jogging in my direction. I dished up his supper and thought about what I wanted to have. I opened the cabinets and found a can of soup that looked promising. No bread for a grilled cheese sandwich, but I found a sleeve of crackers in the back of my chip cabinet. Crackers last forever, right?

Once my soup was done, I sat down and read through my notes while I ate. Something was missing. I just needed to find the connection. I washed up, put my bowl in the dishwasher and headed for bed. Maybe I'd find some answers in my sleep.

* * *

THE INCESSANT RINGING of my cellphone pulled me from a deep, dreamless sleep. It took me a minute to get my bearings as I looked around the room and tried to figure out where the noise was coming from. I hit accept and struggled to stay awake long enough to say hello.

"Brynn, it's Liz Freed."

She sounded rattled. Really rattled. I sat up in bed as my sleepiness evaporated in an instant.

"What's wrong?"

"I just heard from the sheriff up there. Apparently, someone was killed in the cabin. I don't even know why I'm calling you, but I just hung up the phone with the sheriff and you're the first person I thought of. My flight is scheduled for the morning but I don't know what to do.

My tired mind jogged in place for a second until everything clicked into place.

"Oh no, that's terrible. Did you want me to go up there? I know Dave Beldon pretty well. He's a great sheriff."

She let out a shuddering sigh of relief.

"If you could. I'm going to head that way, but it will take me about an hour to get up there. I'd feel better if you could be there."

"Sure, I'll head that way now. Did they give you any details about what happened?"

"No, just that one guest died, and it looked bad. Terrible. My client is going to hit the roof."

I figured now was not the best time to follow-up on my earlier text asking for his contact information. That could keep.

"I'll see you when you get there. Drive safely."

"Thanks, Brynn. I appreciate it more than you know."

I ended the call and ran my fingers through my hair. This was not good. I tossed on a clean pair of jeans and grabbed a hoodie to throw over my tee-shirt. I glanced over at the bed, seeing Bernie looking at me silently.

"I'm going to leave you here, Bernie. There'll be too many people up there."

He nodded his head and curled back up where I'd been sleeping. I looked at my bed longingly and headed down the hall, ready to see what on earth had happened. The night was clear, and I was glad for my hoodie as I pulled out of my driveway. It was going to be really chilly up on the mountain.

I drove up the pass carefully, watching for deer and praying that I wouldn't run into anything. As I turned onto the gravel road leading to the cabin, I could see the night sky was lit up with flashing blue and red lights. Sheriff Dave had quite the crew up here. I parked on the grass, off to the side, so the emergency vehicles could get past me, and walked up to the house.

One deputy stopped me as I approached. His face looked familiar, and it took me a second to remember his name.

"Pete, it's good to see you. Is Dave around?"

His face cleared as he recognized me.

"He's in the back, but I don't know if you should go back there, Miss Brynn. It's not something you'll want to see."

I clapped a hand on his arm and smiled at him.

"It's okay. I'll tell him you warned me."

I walked around the cabin to the back and saw several people clustered around a form on the ground. The emergency medical team was standing near them, shifting on their feet, waiting for the body to be released. Dave heard me walk up behind him and spun on his heels, relaxing when he recognized me.

"Brynn. What are you doing here?"

"Liz Freed called me. She hired me to work on a project up here a few days ago."

"I'm guessing that project has nothing to do with changing out the curtains, does it?"

"I'm afraid not. What happened here?"

"We got a call from the renters," he said, nodding his head towards the glass doors. "This guy here was found when one of them went outside to have a smoke. We're still processing the scene. This has to be one of the worst scenes I've ever worked. It looks like some sort of animal got him."

I looked over at the group of people staring out at us and nodded in their direction. There were quite a few people standing there. I glanced over Dave's shoulder and immediately wished I hadn't. Whoever had died, it hadn't been a good death, and that's all I'm prepared to say on that subject. What was left of my soup threatened to make a re-appearance.

"You don't want to see that, Brynn."

"Is there anything I can do to help?" I asked, feeling out of place.

"Well, unless you can do your thing, I'm not too sure about that right now. I'll want to talk to you in the morning. Well, in a few hours, I guess. I need to know what was going on up here and why you were hired."

"Excuse me, Sheriff Beldon?" Liz Freed asked from behind me.

I turned to look at her, almost doing a double-take. She looked unrecognizable now that she wasn't dressed to the nines in a business suit. Her faded tee and baggy sweatpants made her seem a lot more human and approachable.

"Dave, this is Liz Freed," I said, stepping aside so they could shake hands.

Dave tipped his cowboy hat and gave her a grim look.

"Ms. Freed, I need some information about the people staying here tonight. If you could give the list to one of my deputies, we'll cross reference that information with what the renters have told us."

"Do you think this is going to reflect badly on my client, the owner?" she asked, wringing her hands.

She really seemed to be worked up over how he was going to react. Dave met my eyes, and I quirked an eyebrow.

"Liz, I'm sure he'll understand it's not your fault. It's not like you killed the guy on the ground over there. You didn't kill him, right?"

She looked to where I was pointing and I instantly regretted my gesture. She went white to the mouth and sank to the ground with a little whimper. Dang it.

"Way to go, Brynn," Dave said wryly. "Pete! Where's that blasted deputy?"

"I'm right here, sir," Pete said.

"Can you help Brynn get Ms. Freed out of the way. Once she comes to, I'll need all the information she had on the people renting the cabin."

"Yes, sir. I'll get right on it, sir."

Dave rolled his eyes and turned back to the medical examiner who blessedly covered the body with a sheet. If only he'd done that like a minute ago. I took one of Liz's arms as Pete took the other and between the two of us, we got her tall form sorted out and delivered back to the front porch. I sat her down on a deck chair and rubbed her hands. Her eyes flickered, and she sat bolt upright, looking green around the edges.

I pointed to the side of the deck and she lurched over there, making it just in time. My soup really wanted to join whatever she had for dinner, but I took shallow breaths and tried to keep it together. Pete looked as uncomfortable as I felt and wiped the sweat off his forehead.

"Miss, I hate to bother you, but do you need anything?"

She shook her head and came back to the chair, sinking into it and burying her head in her hands.

"Why did this have to happen?"

I looked at Pete over her head and he shrugged helplessly. I crouched next to Liz and took her hand.

"Liz, it's going to be okay. Now, what can you tell the deputy about the renters? Once you do that, you can head home and get ready for your flight. I'll do what I can to help."

"I'm so sorry. I'm not usually like this. I always have it together. Why am I falling apart?"

She looked at me helplessly.

"Death can impact everyone differently, I guess. Try not to think about it and take deep breaths. I'm sure your client will understand once this is all figured out."

She nodded and obediently took a deep breath while Pete shifted on his feet and stared at his blank notebook. She took the hint and smiled at him as she took out her ponytail and rearranged her hair.

"I'm ready, officer."

"It's Deputy, miss. Do you know who was renting the cabin?"

"Yes," she said, groping for her purse. "I've got the registration information right here. It's all printed out."

"Oh good," Pete said, looking relieved. "I think that's all we need, unless you can think of anything that stood out?"

She shook her head and glanced between us.

"I don't think so. It was a standard group rental."

"Okay, if I have questions, I'll call you. You're free to go."

"Liz, are you okay to drive home?" I asked as she lurched upward from the deep seat of the chair.

"I'm fine," she said, flapping a hand at me. "I'll keep my windows down and the fresh air will help, I think. Will you call me if you find anything else out?"

"I will," I said, unsure of exactly what she wanted me to do, but wanting to help.

She grasped my hand before tottering down the drive towards her gigantic SUV. I glanced over at Pete as he read through the list. The flashing lights from the vehicles were casting strange shadows on the cabin and the trees. The whole thing felt surreal. I tried to shake it off and focus.

"Is there anything I can help you with?" I asked.

He cleared his throat before shaking his head. I put a hand on his arm, feeling bad for the young deputy. This was most likely his first murder scene, and it was not one he'd probably ever forget.

"It will be okay," I said.

He gave me a weak smile and turned to look as the EMTs wheeled the cot with the body past us. Dave brought up the rear and stopped near us.

"Go on inside, Pete. We'll want to question the group."

Pete seemed recharged by having a simple plan of action and he strode inside. I could hear him instructing the renters on how they were going to be questioned. I looked over at Dave.

"Go on home, Brynn. Unless you think this guy's ghost might hang around?"

"I think it's too soon to tell. I'll come back up later on today if that's okay."

He took off his cowboy hat and scrubbed at his thinning hair.

"Sounds good. I'll be in touch later."

"Hey, I'm planning on meeting Zane for lunch at Jill's later today. Do you want to meet up there?"

The mention of Jill's name brought the ghost a smile to his face, and he nodded.

"That'd be just fine."

7

By the time I got home, the first rays of sunlight were just peeking over the hills. I knew trying to go back to sleep was going to be a losing game, so I went straight for the coffeepot. I was going to need a massive amount of caffeine to get through the rest of this day.

I rubbed at my face, trying to shake off the lingering horror of what I'd seen. I'd been quick to dismiss the creature as a living animal, but maybe I'd been too hasty. Was it possible we were dealing with an actual bear? I shook my head as I grabbed a coffee cup and waited for the machine to spit out enough coffee to fill it. No, that just made little sense. Whatever I'd seen vanished, and then coupled with what I'd heard in the attic the day before, it had to be paranormal.

I filled up my mug and took my first sip, wincing as the hot liquid scorched my tongue. I looked over at the sound of a cranky meow and saw Bernie rumpled from sleep and looking like he did not appreciate all the ruckus I was making in the kitchen.

"Sorry, Bernie. I know it's early, but there's no way I could go back to sleep after what I saw," I said with a grimace. "In fact, I may have trouble sleeping tonight if I think too much about it."

I filled him in on the crime scene as I dished up his breakfast and he sat quietly at my feet, whiskers bristling. I placed the bowl on the floor and he wound around my ankles, purring softly.

"Thanks, bud. I don't know what we're going to do about all of this."

I took another sip of my coffee and walked over to the kitchen table to go over my notes again. I'd heard of supernatural creatures scaring people, maybe even scaring them to death, but I never heard of them actually harming anyone physically.

I walked into the living room and flipped on the television to catch the early morning news. It was rare for something like this to happen in our small community, and I was betting the larger news station in Rapid Falls was going to cover it, and I wasn't disappointed. A reporter was on the scene and I could see Dave in the distance, looking unhappily at the camera. I turned up the volume as Bernie joined me on the couch, snuggling on top of my feet.

"I'm here on the scene of a chilling murder in the popular mountain resort community near Coppertown. So far, the authorities have released no information on the victim, but it appears the person was part of a large group of vacationers who were staying in this cabin. Sheriff Beldon, do you have anything to add for our viewers?"

I quirked a smile at the look on Dave's face as he listened to the reporter. His hat was pushed back on his head and his thumbs were looped through his duty belt.

"This is an ongoing investigation. The victim's family needs to be noti-fied. We'll have an official statement for the press later this morning."

Dave turned to leave, and the reporter chased after him, putting a hand on his arm.

"Sheriff, do you have anything further to add?"

Dave looked down at the reporter's hand on his arm and removed it, handling the appendage like it was a dead fish.

"As I just said, we'll have an official statement for you later. That's all."

The reporter turned back to the camera and droned on. My eyes felt heavy as I listened to him wrap up his report. The sound of an engine interrupted him and a pickup truck skidded into view of the camera. My eyes flew open at this recent development. The door opened and a tall man got out and slammed the door before stalking towards the cabin.

"Sir, do you know anything about what happened here?"

The reporter chased after the man, who turned and gave him a look of disdain. His handsome face twisted into a snarl.

"I'm the owner. I just got here. Do I look like I know anything?"

The reporter turned back to the camera and wrapped up his report, throwing it back to the station. I turned the volume back down and looked at Bernie.

"What did you make of all of that?"

He let out a sigh and snuggled his head closer to my feet. I stroked his black fur, admiring the way it gleamed in the early morning sunshine.

"I hear you. I feel the same way."

I tried to focus on the rest of the news, but eventually, I must have nodded off. The next thing I was aware of was my phone ringing and a serious crink in my neck. I groped for my phone on the table and answered it.

"Sullivan Staging."

"Copper Top! Did I wake you? It's nearly ten in the morning. You sleeping on the job?" Logan asked, his voice booming through the phone.

I winced as I struggled into a more comfortable position. Bernie stretched and went to the far end of the couch, giving me a reproachful look before settling into place.

"It was a long night," I said, running a hand through my hair.

"Did Zane stay over?" Logan asked, snickering.

"Oh geez, get your mind out of the gutter. No, there was a killing at the cabin I told you about. I went up there early this morning, but there wasn't much I could do."

"Brynn, what do you mean?"

"You haven't seen the news?"

"Duh, I've been working since six. I've got to get this project done. What happened?"

I told Logan about what I'd seen up at the cabin and on the news.

"Ew, that sounds gross. Do you think the guy got mauled by an animal?"

"I'm not sure, but it was bad. I hope I never have to see anything like that again."

"Are you okay?" he asked, sounding more serious. "That couldn't have been pleasant seeing that."

"I'm fine. I'm sure whoever died found the experience way more unpleasant than I did."

"You're gonna let Dave solve this one, right? There's no need for you to get involved now. You were hired to see if something supernatural was going on, not solve a gruesome murder."

"Yeah, that sounds nothing like me. Of course I'm going to be involved. I think there's a lot more going on than we know. I've got to figure it out."

"Brynn..."

"I'll be fine. The owner seems interesting. I'm hoping I'll be able to talk to him today. I think there might be a link between one of his ancestors and what's happening up there."

"I don't like it. I know telling you to stay out of it will only make you more interested, but still."

"It will be okay."

"If you say so. Anyway, the reason I called was to let you know you'll be able to get in and do your design thing later in the week up here at the hotel. My guys should have all the renovations done in the next two days."

"Sweet! I'll get everything organized."

"Want to go out tonight with me and Kels? We can double date, or you can third-wheel."

"That sounds like fun," I said with a snort. "Nothing like being a third wheel."

"I kid. But seriously, do you want to go out with us? We're planning on having Mexican. I've never known you to turn down a taco. I'll even buy."

"Free tacos? I'm tempted, but I think this girl is gonna be out like a light before eight tonight. I barely slept."

"Well, think about it and let me know."

"Will do," I said, not even trying to stifle an enormous yawn.

Logan chuckled.

"My cousin is so ladylike."

"Whatever."

I made a rude noise and signed off, ending the call and stretching out my kinks. I looked at the remains of my cold cup of coffee and wandered into the kitchen to pour it out and get a refill. As I sipped on the sweet caffeine juice, I thought about what I wanted to do for the rest of the day. First things first. I needed a shower to banish the cobwebs from my brain. After that, I'd have lunch with Zane and see if I could track down the owner of the cabin. Feeling like I had a plan, I hopped in the shower and washed away most of my tiredness.

My phone dinged with a text as I was getting dressed. Zane was on his way up to Jill's, giving me just enough time to finish getting ready. I shouted for Bernie on my way out the door, but he barely raised his head from the couch. Wishing I could nap for a few more hours, I shook my head and walked out into the sunshine. The sky was a beautiful shade of blue and there were just a few wisps of clouds in the sky.

I made it to Jill's before Zane and parked to wait for him to show up. I pulled out my phone and dialed Liz's number. She hadn't mentioned when her flight was leaving and I hoped I could catch her before she left. It rang several times before forwarding to voicemail. I frowned and left a quick message, asking for the information on the owner of the cabin. As I ended the call, Zane's Jeep pulled in front of me and parked. He got out and gave me a smile that made my knees shake a little. I slid out of my car and joined him on the sidewalk.

"Hello, beautiful. How's my girl, today?"

He leaned over and kissed me on the cheek, pulling me into his side. I snuggled close and sighed. Heaven, I tell you, pure bliss. We walked into Jill's, grabbed two menus, and headed for our favorite booth. I looked around for Dave, but it didn't look like he'd made it in yet. Jill spotted us and gave a shout and a wave as she bustled between tables, carrying her ever-present coffee pot.

I looked around the 1950s themed restaurant and smiled. This was one of my favorite places on earth. Jill had decorated it to match an old diner, right down to the red vinyl booths and chairs. It was like stepping back in time to a simpler place, especially when you glimpsed Jill wearing a twin-set and a matching poodle skirt, complete with bobby socks and saddle shoes. The woman had style to spare. I looked into Zane's eyes and smiled as the corners of his eyes wrinkled as his icy blue eyes met mine.

"How was your night?" I asked, looking through the menu, even though I already knew it by heart.

He sighed and tucked a strand of hair behind his ear.

"Long. It took me way longer than I expected to get all the hidden cameras installed. The good thing is, by tonight, we should have a better idea of what's going on in there. No one came in last night while I was working. I half hoped they would so I could go home early. I hope you had a good night's sleep at least."

I snorted as I reached across the table to grab his hand.

"Not so much."

He raised his eyebrow, and I launched into my tale of the events from earlier in the day. He frowned as he listened, a worry line appearing in between his brows. I wanted to smooth it away. I just finished as Jill walked up, ready to take our order. She looked at me closely and shook her head.

"No bacon cheeseburger for you today, missy. You look like you need some comfort food. You're getting the roast beef and mashed potatoes with gravy."

My stomach came to life with an embarrassingly loud growl and I couldn't help but laugh.

"Looks like my stomach agrees with you. Let's do it."

"With your usual Coke, of course. And for you, handsome?"

Jill smiled at Zane as his handsome face blushed. He was so easy to tease and she took advantage of that every time she saw him. He cleared his throat.

"I'll have the same thing."

She gave a brisk nod and turned to me.

"You okay, sugar? Dave called me earlier. Sounds like nasty business up there."

"Is he still planning on stopping by for lunch? I was hoping to talk to him."

She nodded as someone called out for a refill of coffee.

"Hold your dang horses, Jimmy. I'll be right there," she said, shouting over her shoulder. "He should be here in about five minutes. I'll get him the same thing you're having and have it all come out together, if that's fine?"

"That sounds perfect. Thanks, Jill."

She sailed off, yelling our order at the kitchen before walking over to the thirsty Jimmy. I met Zane's eyes and my heart leapt into my throat when I saw the concern mirrored in them.

"I don't know about this, Brynn. It sounds like you're dealing with way more than just a simple ghost."

"I don't know. I think there's something going on that can't be explained. I need more information."

"Maybe I can help with that," Dave said as he slid into the booth next to Zane. "Howdy, Zane."

"Hi, Dave. Jill already ordered for you."

Dave gave a small smile and looked over his shoulder at Jill. She paused in her whirlwind rounds and winked at him, making the old cowboy blush a little. They were just the cutest. My inner matchmaker let out a cheer and I stifled my grin before Dave turned back to look at me.

"I saw that, young lady."

"I know you did. It just makes me happy seeing you two."

His blush deepened and I changed the subject, not wanting him to feel too uncomfortable.

"I saw you on the news. The owner of the cabin looked like a piece of work. What's he like?" I asked.

"He's something else. He's not from here, that's for sure. He was shouting about wanting a CSI team up there and immediate results. As if our little department has a CSI team."

Zane sat back in the booth and looked over at Dave.

"Is there anything I can help with? I know it wouldn't be on an official basis, but I have some experience that might come in handy."

Zane was in the military for several tours before taking early retirement and coming to live in Golden Hills. He never talked much about his background, and while I knew he was dealing with a few ghosts of his own, I didn't push him. He would tell me more when he was ready. Dave looked at Zane seriously and nodded.

"Might take you up on that. We're spread pretty thin as it is. Pete's a good deputy, but he's used to dealing with wayward animal calls and traffic stops."

"Whatever you need, I'll help."

"Might bring you on as a consultant or something. Wouldn't pay much."

"I don't care about the money. I just want to keep this one safe," Zane said, pointing over at me. "And if I know anything about her, she will not back down. I'd feel better if I could watch over her."

"Hey, I'm right here," I said, not liking where this conversation was going.

Dave snorted and removed his cowboy hat, putting it on the table, crown down.

"I'm very aware of that. And I like where you're going with this, Zane."

I glanced between them and chewed on my lip. On the one hand, getting to work closer with Zane would be awesome. On the other, I didn't appreciate being babysat. I was saved from further contemplation by our food. My stomach let out another groan as Jill slid the plate of roast beef in front of me.

"If this looks half as good as it smells, it's gonna be amazing," Dave said, taking a reverent sniff.

"Eat up, cowboy," Jill said, with a wink. "You too, handsome.

You're both going to need your strength if you're gonna keep up with this one."

She jerked her thumb in my direction before letting out a cackle and heading off to another table. Dave and Zane exchanged glances and started chuckling. I was too busy heaping roast beef and mashed potatoes on my fork to reply, which was probably a good thing.

8

J ill was absolutely right. The comfort food made me feel about a thousand percent better and I was recharged and ready to get to work. As we walked back to our cars, I had a thought. I wasn't sure if Dave would go for it, but I figured it wouldn't hurt to ask.

"Dave, do you mind if I interview the other people who were at the cabin last night? I know you took their statements, but I'm wondering if they might be more open with me."

Dave readjusted his hat and looked at me keenly for a second before nodding.

"Heck, why not. It won't hurt anything. I think I'd leave them be for today, though. The management company said they would move them to another cabin since they can't stay at the scene. I bet the tall gal could tell you where they're at. We've asked them not to leave town for the next few days as a precaution. They weren't thrilled about it."

"I'll ask Liz. Do you have any information about the man who died?"

Dave frowned and unwrapped the toothpick he'd grabbed from the counter at Jill's. He rolled it around his mouth for a few seconds.

"As long as it goes no further, his name was Sean Treadwell. We're still trying to track down his family. Do you think you'll be able to find his, well, his ghost?" Dave asked, looking uncomfortable as he squinted at me.

"There's a good chance his soul might still be around. That was a traumatic death if I've ever seen one. Is it okay if I go back to the cabin? I'll avoid anything you've taped off."

"That's fine," Dave said, turning to Zane. "As for you, are you sure you want to be a consultant?"

Zane nodded and wrapped his arm around me.

"I'd love to help. I do need to finish up a few things on this job I'm working on, but as of tomorrow, I'll be able to help."

"I'll take you up on that. Stop by the county building in the morning and we'll get you set up with some official paperwork," Dave said before taking the toothpick out of his mouth and jabbing it in my direction. "You stay out of trouble, hear? I'm pretty fond of you and I'd hate to see you get in over your head. We're still waiting on a cause of death."

"I'm guessing getting ripped to shreds isn't an official finding, huh?" I asked.

Dave grimaced and put his hand over his stomach.

"Don't remind me. I'll be in touch."

He walked down the street towards his pickup, and I glanced up at Zane. He was looking down at me with a smile, eyes crinkled up.

"Are you going to listen to the Sheriff and stay out of trouble?"

"Define trouble," I said with a laugh.

He kissed me softly and rested his forehead against mine.

"I think you know exactly what I mean, Brynn. If you need anything, call me. I'm only a few minutes away. Starting tomorrow, I'll be able to help. We can interview the people from the cabin together."

"I enjoy working with you," I said, bopping him gently on the nose with mine before stepping back. "I'm going to track down the owner, maybe stop by the cabin to see if poor Sean's ghost is around, and then I think I'll head home. I need an early night after this morning."

"I'll call you later," Zane said as he opened my car door for me. "Later, Sullivan."

"Later, Matthews."

I looked at my phone before turning on the ignition. Liz had come through for me. Score! She'd sent a text with the owner's number, and a plea to tread lightly around him. Judging from what I'd seen on the news, I could see why. He didn't seem like the nicest person. Maybe that was why she was so freaked out about him finding out. I sent a text back asking if she had the address for where the other renters were staying while the investigation continued. I planned to be up there first thing in the morning, after Zane talked to Dave.

I dialed the number she sent and a man's voice answered on the second ring.

"This is Trent."

"Hi, Trent. My name is Brynn Sullivan. I don't know if Liz Freed mentioned she hired me to look into a few things that were going on at your cabin?"

He snorted and barked out a coughing laugh.

"Fat lot of good that did me. Yeah, she mentioned you in passing. What do you want?"

I tried to shake off his attitude and soldiered on, determined to ignore his rudeness.

"I was wondering if you could spare a few minutes to talk about the cabin? I have a couple questions."

"You and everyone else in this godforsaken place. I don't know why I moved to this stupid area. The cops are useless and I get amateur ghost hunters bothering me, on top of dead bodies."

"I won't take much of your time. Do you have an office locally?"

He let out a sigh that suggested he was more than done with this conversation before replying curtly.

"Fine. My office is in Creekside. I'll be here for another hour, so you better make it quick. I'll text you the address."

He ended the call, and I stared at my phone for a second, waiting for his text. Right. Creekside was about twenty minutes away, so I needed to hurry if I didn't want to miss him. I started up my car and headed down the highway, praying traffic would be light. We were still hanging on to the tail edges of summer and tourists were everywhere.

I made it with about a half hour to spare and found a place to park that was about a block down from his office. I resisted looking into the shop windows as I passed, knowing I couldn't afford to get distracted by cool antiques. I was always on the lookout for pieces that would work with my interior design projects, but right now was not the time to shop. I walked into the office and looked around. It was a spartan space, and there was an empty spot where I expected a receptionist's desk to be.

"Hello? Trent?"

"Back here."

I headed down a hallway and found Trent sitting at a beautifully carved mahogany desk. My fingers itched to touch it, but something about the look on his face told me that wouldn't be appreciated or tolerated. I sat across from him and pasted on a bright smile, hoping I could wear down his defenses with cheer.

"Thanks so much for agreeing to see me," I said, holding my hand across the desk for him to shake.

He looked even more handsome in person, but his face was marred with an ugly frown that pulled his eyebrows towards his nose. He looked at my hand for a second before grudgingly giving it a limp shake.

"What do you want to know?"

He leaned back in his chair and steepled his hands over his stomach.

"I'm looking into the history of the cabin to see if I can find anything that would explain the strange occurrences that have been taking place. Do you know anything about it?"

"Nope. Saw the place a few months ago on a property site and figured it would be an excellent investment. I moved here from Colorado at the first of the year."

"Welcome to the hills," I said, still trying to charm him out of his funk.

He snorted and rolled his eyes.

"Yeah, right? I've got to get going. You've got exactly five minutes."

"Were you aware that one of the first owners of the property shared your last name?"

He blinked and looked to the side before answering.

"I was not. It's a common enough name. Why are you bothering me with this minutia? It's obvious one of the other cabin owners is butthurt they lost out on the deal of a lifetime with that place and now they're trying to smear my name. I didn't think they'd stoop to murder though."

"Deal of a lifetime?"

"Yeah, I got that place for a song. Most of the cabins up there are worth half a million or more. I got that place for two hundred. I almost wish I hadn't bought it. It hasn't been worth the hassle, that's for sure."

"Do you think any of the other property owners have a serious enough grudge against you they'd commit a gruesome murder?"

"Who knows? Everyone around here is an inbred local or a cutthroat investor."

This guy was a real charmer. I struggled to stay positive.

"Do you own a lot of properties?"

He sighed and pushed back from his desk, pulling himself up to his full height.

"Just two, so far. My other cabin is off another side road on the mountain. I'm waiting to see how profitable they are before I sink more money in. I might not stick around. The sheriff was saying I can't rent that place back out for at least another two weeks, so I'm just losing money. At least I have the other place, so I didn't have to refund this group's rental fees. Now, if that's everything, I need to go."

It wasn't everything, not by a long shot. His answers just created more questions. My mind raced as I stood up, trying to figure out one more good question. I stood up to leave and paused in the doorway.

"Does your other property have any similar issues?"

He cocked his head at me before shaking it.

"No, it's been fine."

He walked me to the door in the lobby and I stopped as he opened it.

"What brought you here from Colorado?"

"Fewer people, similar scenery, cheap properties."

"I see. Well, thanks for your time. I hope everything turns around for you."

He sneered and slammed the door behind me. Okay, then. I walked back to my car, antique furniture completely forgotten as I thought about his interview. He was lying when he said he wasn't aware a past owner had the same name. But why? I groaned as I got behind the wheel, feeling my lack of sleep catch up to me.

I got back on the highway and headed for the cabin. With any luck, the scene was already processed, and I'd have the place to myself. I wasn't sure if the ghost of Sean Treadwell would hang around, but it was worth a shot.

By the time I made it back up the mountain, the light was fading as the sun sank in the west. I got out of my car and rubbed my arms, wishing I'd kept my hoodie from earlier. There weren't any cars parked out front, which I took to be a good sign. There was still police tape on the doors of the cabin, so I walked around the back of the cabin and looked at the patch of grass where Sean's body was found.

A blood splotch was still visible on the grass and I swallowed hard, remembering the scene from this morning. Now, it was quiet and almost peaceful, as birds chirped and the wind whispered through the pine trees. I sat on the steps of the deck and looked around, trying to quiet my mind.

For a second, I thought I saw a faint figure standing in the taped off section. I stayed still and waited, hoping the figure would become more solid. I breathed quietly through my nose and blinked. Still there. That was a good sign. I tried making contact.

"Sean?"

The figure turned towards me and wavered around the edges.

"Who are you?"

"My name is Brynn Sullivan. I'd like to help. Are you Sean?"

"That name sounds familiar. Everything is all jumbled up. Did I fall and hit my head or something? All I remember is darkness and then coming to standing here. I should go back inside."

His translucent form turned towards me and walked through the tape. He came to a stop and looked at me.

"Sean, I don't know how to tell you this," I said, trying to find the most diplomatic way to break the awful news to him.

"What's going on? Why is everything so dark around the edges? I must have hit my head really hard."

I tried a different angle.

"What was the last thing you remember?"

He wavered around the edges, almost disappearing, and I knew I needed to work quickly. It was difficult for newer ghosts to maintain their presence on this side. I wasn't sure why that was, but it seemed to be a universal rule. My ghostly friend, Charles Thurgood, was a master at staying nearly solid for hours at a time, but he had plenty of practice since he'd passed on in the 1920s.

"I remember looking at these trees," he said, pointing towards the forest. "Why am I here? Everything is all jumbled up in my head. I need a drink."

He walked towards me, fading with each step.

"Sean, wait."

He stepped onto the deck and the hair on my arms stood up as he got closer and the temperature dipped. He tried to put his hand on the railing and looked at me with panic in his eyes when his hand passed right through the wood.

"Lady, I don't know who you are, but this is whacked. Am I dreaming? That must be it. I'm asleep and having a crazy dream."

"I hate to be the one to tell you this, and I know it won't be easy to hear. You passed on early this morning. I'm trying to help the sheriff figure out who killed you."

"What? No. I'm not dead. I'm asleep. I'm going to wake up any second and laugh about all of this."

He shook his head back and forth quickly, becoming almost entirely transparent. I only had a few seconds left to communicate with him. I reached out on instinct, wishing I could comfort him. He watched as my hand slid through his arm and let out a squeaky scream.

"I need to wake up, I need to wake up."

And with that, he disappeared. I let out a sigh, frustrated that I couldn't get through to him. It was so hard to be the one to tell someone they were no longer among the living, especially when they died suddenly. I walked down the steps and turned to leave when the hair on the back of my neck stood up. It felt like someone was watching me. I paused as I peered through the trees. A faint cackle sounded, and I zeroed in a spot close to the deck where there were overgrown shrubs.

"Poor sucker," a voice said.

"Who's here?" I asked, resisting the urge to walk closer to the voice.

I reasoned with myself that whatever was talking was obviously not a bear, trying to calm the panic that was clawing at my spine. Had I finally contacted the creature?

Whatever it was gave a startled snort, and the shrubs rattled as something moved within.

"I can hear you," I said. "Is your name Edward?"

I was making a leap that the creature was indeed the ghost of Edward Davis, and I crossed my fingers, hoping I was right. A hush descended in the yard and I almost gave up hope of finding an answer when the scratchy voice sounded again.

"They called me Ned."

A powerful wind swept through the trees and I could hear branches cracking. I craned my neck, trying to see what was happening as the sounds grew further away.

"Ned?"

Nothing. I waited a few more minutes before giving up and

heading towards the driveway This was a different kind of ghost, that was for sure. As I got in my car, I thought about what it could all mean. I shook my head as I drove back down the mountain. I needed to get home and catch up on some sleep. Tomorrow was another day and hopefully it would bring some much needed answers.

9

A good night's sleep made all the difference. I poured myself
another cup of coffee and brushed my hand over Bernie's back
as he enjoyed his breakfast. Liz answered my text from the day before
and I saved the address into my mapping app so we could find it
easily. I checked the time on the microwave and smiled when I heard
a familiar engine cut off in front of my house. Zane wasn't wasting
time this morning. I opened the front door and smiled as he walked
towards me. Partially because he was hotter than the sun and
partially because he was carrying a big box of what appeared to be
donuts. I took a big sniff. Yep, fresh donuts. He caught me sniffing and
broke out into a laugh.

"I think I know the way to your heart," he said, leaning down to
give me a kiss on the cheek.

"I'm practical, if nothing else. Are those from the new bakery in
Deadwood?"

"They are, milady. I brought a box to Dave and his deputies, too."

He opened the box, and I let out a gigantic sigh of appreciation.
He'd chosen a variety pack and I couldn't figure out which one I
wanted to try first. I looked over at Zane and he gave me an encour-

aging nod. I picked the cherry danish and sunk my teeth into a little piece of heaven. I kept from groaning, but it was a close thing.

Zane grabbed an iced maple donut as I poured him a cup of coffee.

"How was Dave?" I asked after I finally swallowed my enormous bite of danish.

"He seemed a little stressed. The family wants some answers and I know he does, too. Hopefully, the coroner's report will help."

"Are you officially a consultant, now?"

He nodded as he took another bite of his donut, polishing it off. A man after my heart.

"So, what do you want to do first?"

"Let's interview the other people in Sean's group and see what they have to say. With any luck, one of them saw or heard something that might be important."

Bernie chirped at my feet and I pinched off a small section of my danish for him, feeling bad that I couldn't bring him with me. He purred his appreciation and disappeared into the living room with his treat. I brushed the icing off my hands and grabbed my bag, looking longingly at the box on the counter. One was fine for now, but I had plans for the rest of those delicious creations later.

"I'll drive, unless you wanted to take separate vehicles."

"No, let's take the one. Have you ever been to the resort area?"

I locked the door behind me as we walked out.

"I haven't. I'm looking forward to it. You mentioned a few weeks ago that it's pretty fun to ski up there."

"I love it," I said. "I mean, it's not like the mountains in Colorado, but the runs are fun and they've got good hot chocolate."

Zane chuckled as we got into his Jeep. It was spotless on the inside and I was glad I hadn't brought a donut for the road. With my luck, I would've gotten crumbs everywhere. I gave Zane directions, and he nodded.

"So, did you learn anything interesting after lunch?"

As we drove, I told him about my experience meeting the owner and then running into the ghost of Sean Treadwell. His eyebrow went up like a flag when I got to the part about Edward's ghost.

"You really think it's him, then? Not a ghost bear?"

I shook my head and laughed.

"No, he's not a ghost bear. I wish I could have talked longer with him. I'd love to understand how he's able to manipulate his environment."

"Do what now?"

"He can move branches and make noises that most ghosts can't. It's something entirely new to me."

Zane blanched as we headed up the mountain and shot a quick look over at me.

"You don't mean like a poltergeist or anything, do you? I saw that movie and that's going to be a hard no from me if that's what we're dealing with."

"No, silly. I don't think he's a poltergeist. Or at least I hope he's not."

"Not helping."

"He doesn't seem to have the anger necessary to be that kind of spirit. Although whatever I heard in the attic was sure angry. I don't know if that was him or if we're dealing with multiple entities."

"Okay, that's really not helping."

"It will be fine. Besides, we're focusing mostly on interviewing the rest of the group. Depending on how long that takes, we may not even have time to stop by the other cabin. I'd like to get your opinion on how you feel there, though."

Zane swallowed hard and tried to smile at me. I rubbed his arm and gave him an encouraging smile. He was new to all of this, but at least he was keeping an open mind. We pulled to a stop in front of the cabin where the group was now staying.

"I'll let you take the lead, but I may jump in if I have any follow-ups."

"Perfect. Let's see what we can find out."

Zane knocked on the door of the cabin and it took a few seconds before we heard a shout from the inside.

"Coming."

A pretty woman swung open the door and blinked at us.

"You're not our food delivery."

"No, sorry," I said. "I'm Brynn Sullivan and this is Zane Matthews, a consultant with the sheriff's department. Did Liz let you know we'd be coming up to ask a few questions?"

She nodded absently and looked over my shoulder, as if wishing a delivery person was going to materialize. I followed her line of sight and shrugged.

"I guess. Come on in. Everybody's in the living room."

"How many of you are up here?"

"Six. Well, I guess it's five now. I still can't believe what happened."

We followed her into the living room and I glanced around, trying to get a read on everyone.

"Hi," I said, trying to break the ice as four sets of eyes stared at us. "We won't take too much of your time, but we have a few questions, if that's okay."

A man slouched on the couch let out a disbelieving snort.

"More questions? Geez, haven't we suffered enough already? We're all terrified of leaving this cabin. Any of us could be the next victim of that vicious creature."

The other man on the couch nodded at me and I glanced over at the beautiful girl perched on a chair. She looked lost and my heart went out to her. I recognized the signs of grief and would've put money on her being closer to Sean Treadwell than the others.

"You'll have to excuse Seth," the girl who let us in said as she slapped him on the shoulder after wedging herself next to him on the couch. "This has all been a lot to take in. I'm sure that was a random animal attack. Have you heard if they've caught it yet?"

"I know the sheriff is working hard on solving the case," I said, not wanting to say any more than that.

"Pshh. Barney Fife and the gang. Yeah, a lot's gonna get done with that crew. For all we know, there's a rabid bear out there hunting people down, one by one," the other man on the couch said.

"God, Trevor. Don't be so rude," said the girl in between them. "Sorry, we're all really rattled."

Zane and I sat across from the group on the loveseat and I tried to smile encouragingly.

"If it's okay with you, we'll go one by one. If you could tell us your names, and then describe what happened before you found Sean."

The girl on the chair let out a sob and ran from the room. Seth rolled his eyes and gave me a look.

"That was Trish. She's Sean's girlfriend. Or was, I guess. Sorry, this has been a lot to take in," he said.

He paused as he rubbed his forehead.

"It's okay. I know this is difficult. What's your last name?" I asked.

"Grand. Seth Grand. I knew Sean throughout college. We all did. We graduated last year, and this was our first couple's trip since then."

"Do you all live in the same area?" Zane asked.

"Yeah, we're from Riverton, on the east side of the state."

"Were all of you pretty close?" I asked.

Trevor let out a snort and Seth glared over at him before nodding at me.

"Yeah, we knew each other pretty well. I can't believe Sean's gone. It just doesn't seem possible."

"Can you describe what took place last night?"

Seth rubbed his forehead again and looked off towards the kitchen as a tall girl wandered over and took the chair Trish left.

"It was a normal night. We'd gotten checked in and were figuring out our plans for the evening. Trevor here wanted to go into town and check out the casinos, but the rest of us were shot. We stayed in and the girls cooked up a feast. After that, we hung out and did our own thing. I went to bed early with Willow," he said, nodding at the girl who'd let us in.

"You heard nothing strange? Was it normal for Sean to separate himself from the group?"

Seth paused before he answered, glancing over at Trevor.

"Sometimes. I always struggle to sleep in a new environment, so I took a sleeping pill. Sorry, that's all I remember. I went to bed and the next thing I know the girls were screaming and it was chaos."

I turned my attention to the other man on the couch.

"Trevor, was it?" I asked.

He gave a sullen nod and looked at his watch.

"How long is that food going to take? I should have just made breakfast."

"You mean I should've made it," the tall girl in the chair said, looking up from her hair that she was examining in the morning light.

"Whatever. You guys are better cooks. But, yeah, I'm Trevor Porter. Sean was my best friend."

I looked over at Seth and then back at Trevor.

"I thought Seth said you two didn't always get along?"

Trevor smirked and raised a shoulder.

"That's our dynamic. We're best buds, though. We went to high school together and then to the same college. We were tight."

The girl on the chair snorted, and I turned to her.

"I'm sorry, I didn't catch your name."

She tucked her long hair over her shoulder and glanced down at her fingernails, picking at them.

"I'm Violet Deets."

"Did you know Sean well, too?"

Trevor let out another snort and glared at the girl before looking away.

"As well as I could, I guess. I'm Trevor's girlfriend, so whenever they hang out, I'd see him."

"Violet didn't like Sean," Trevor said. "She was always hassling me about spending too much time with him and not focusing on our relationship."

He ended the last part of his statement with air quotes that somehow dripped with sarcasm. I raised an eyebrow and glanced over at Zane. This was not a relationship that was built for the long haul, if I had to guess about it.

"Is that true, Violet?"

She shrugged and went back to examining her hair.

"He was alright. I didn't really care."

"Yeah, right," Trevor said.

"Did you hear anything last night?" Zane asked.

Trevor let out a gusty sigh and shook his head.

"I had a few drinks before I went to bed. I was out like a light."

"A few? More like most of a case," Violet said with a sneer. "You were snoring so loud I couldn't sleep. I had to sleep on the couch."

I zeroed in on her.

"How about you? If you were in the living room, that would've been close to where Sean was found. Did you hear anything?"

She briefly made eye contact before returning her attention to her hair. Geez, this girl was super worried about split ends.

"No, I didn't hear a thing. Once I was away from the snorer here, I finally fell asleep. The next thing I knew, Trish was screaming so loud it about gave me a heart attack."

"I see. How about you, Willow?"

I turned back to the girl on the couch and she shrugged, shaking her head.

"I heard nothing. I was exhausted. I'd been up half the night before packing and crashed next to this guy here," she said, rubbing Seth's leg. "I sleep really hard. I don't understand it, though. How could our friend get killed right outside the cabin and none of us heard anything? No screams? I know if a wild animal got me, I'd scream my head off."

She made eye contact with me and I sensed she was truly puzzled.

"Did any of you notice anything off about Sean? Did he seem worried about anything that night?"

"No, he was his usual self. He was always the life of the party, trying to get everyone to get along," Seth said, shaking his head. "Now he's dead."

I looked over at Zane and nodded my head in the direction Seth's girlfriend went. He nodded, understanding what I meant, and turned back to the group. I stood up and headed down the hall. I could hear Zane asking a few more questions as I knocked on the closed door.

"Trish? Is it okay if I come in?" I asked.

She opened the door, rubbing her nose with the back of her hand, and stepped aside so I could enter. She went back to the bed, moving like a zombie, and grabbed a tissue before sitting down on it, crossing her legs.

"Sorry, I just couldn't take being in the same room with them," she said..

"I understand. How long were you and Sean together? This has to be difficult."

She wiped her eyes before answering.

"Five years. I thought when he suggested this cabin that he was going to propose. I'd waited so long. I didn't know it was going to be a group vacation until right before we left."

"Did that upset you?"

She huffed a laugh and looked at me.

"A little," she said, raising a shoulder briefly. "I mean, we see these guys all the time back home. I didn't see why we needed to take a vacation with them, too."

"What was Sean like? Seth said he was the life of the party."

She looked out the window and appeared lost in thought for a few seconds.

"He was. He was bigger than life. Always ready with a laugh and a joke. I can't believe I won't hear his laugh ever again."

I sat next to her on the bed and put a hand on her arm, wishing I could comfort her.

"They said you were the one who found him?"

She nodded and her breath hitched.

"I woke up, and he wasn't next to me. I went to the kitchen, figuring he'd gotten hungry. He was always sneaking leftovers after dinner. He wasn't there, though. I looked around and then went outside, thinking maybe he'd gone out to sit on the deck. He always enjoyed being outside. That's when... that's when I saw him."

She broke down in sobbing cries and I put my arms around her.

She cried for a few minutes and I grabbed the box of tissues for her.

"I'm so sorry, Trish. I know how hard this must be for you."

"I just don't know what to do. He was my life, my future. We've lived together for three years. What am I supposed to do now?"

I tucked her hair behind her ear and rubbed her arm.

"You have to go on. It's the hardest thing to do. Even though you've lost someone you loved, you're still living and you've got to keep on doing that. I'm not saying it will be easy, but the pain will lessen. You'll remember his smile, and his laugh, and you'll keep going, day by day."

She looked at me and cocked her head.

"It sounds like you know a lot about grief."

"I do. I'm sorry you had to go through this."

"Thanks. If it's okay, I'd like to be alone for a bit."

"No problem. I appreciate you talking with me."

I closed the door softly behind me and went back into the living room. Zane was standing by the loveseat, waiting for me. The other four were clustered in the kitchen, unpacking their food that must have just arrived. Willow noticed me and came around the counter.

"Is she okay?"

"I think she just needs some time. I'd check on her soon. Maybe keep her food warm for her. She needs to eat, even if she says she's not hungry."

"I'll look after her. I'm sorry I couldn't be of more help. All I remember is waking up to Trish's screams. I don't think I'll ever forget that."

I dug in my bag for a card and handed it to her.

"If you think of anything else, call me?"

She took my card and slipped it into the pocket of her jeans.

"I will."

I followed Zane outside and took a deep breath as we walked back to the Jeep.

"Well, that was interesting," he said as he put the Jeep in gear. "Where to now?"

"Let's head over to the cabin and see if we can find Sean."

10

As Zane drove to the cabin, I noticed the blue skies were turning a shadowy gray, and pulled out my phone to check the weather. I loaded the app, but it just sat there and refused to update. No signal. Darn it. Hopefully, it would hold off until we got down the hill. At least we were in Zane's Jeep and if it did rain, his tires would be more than capable of handling the slick mountain road. I put my phone back and turned to Zane.

"What did you ask them when I was talking to Trish?"

"Just a few questions. I wanted to nail down why they all went to bed and didn't seem to notice that one of their friends was missing. What did Trish have to say?"

"Not much. I didn't want to press her too hard. She seemed really broken up about it. Apparently, she was expecting to get engaged over the weekend, until she found out it was a group vacation."

"Huh, that's interesting. Is this the right road?"

I checked the sign and nodded. The roads up here were like a maze if you weren't used to them.

"What did you make out of their reactions?"

Zane frowned and looked in his rearview mirror before glancing over at me.

"Honestly? They seemed really focused on the wild animal angle. That one guy, Trevor, he's just got a poor attitude. I don't think he's that upset Sean's gone."

"Really? Do you think he might have killed him?"

"I'm not sure, but there was definitely something going on between them. Why did he get so wasted? If you believe what his girlfriend said, I guess."

"Drinking that much seems excessive, but that might just be his norm. It's hard to tell. The cabin's right up ahead."

"What did you think of Violet?"

"The girl with the split ends? I don't know. I sensed a lot of veiled hostility. Honestly, the whole dynamic between everyone was kinda weird. With friends like those people..."

"Who needs enemies?"

"Exactly. Well, here we are," I said, opening the door and sliding out. "I'll be interested to see what you think of this place."

Zane followed me up to the door, and I punched in the code Liz gave me earlier. It worked, and the lock popped open. I opened the door and walked in, taking a sniff as I remembered the powerful stink I'd experienced the last time I'd been here. Thankfully, it wasn't present. I'd forgotten to ask the group if they'd noticed anything odd when they were up here and cursed softly under my breath. Zane turned to look at me.

"What's wrong?"

"Oh, I just should have asked if any of them heard or smelled anything odd while they were here."

He wrinkled up his nose and my heart skipped a beat. He was just so darn attractive.

"Let's hope we don't get a repeat performance. Besides, I'm not sure you would've gotten the truth out of them, anyway."

"I think Willow is honest. The others? Not so sure. Do you want to see the back deck where Sean was found?"

He paused and tucked his hair behind his ear.

"Do you think Sean's ghost will be around?"

"He might be. It's hard to tell with newer ghosts. They struggle to control their environment and it's difficult for them. They pop in and out unexpectedly."

"What about the poltergeist?"

I opened the sliding door.

"I don't think Ned's a poltergeist."

The wind picked up as we walked back outside and stood on the deck. The tops of the trees were bending back and forth, and I could hear branches snapping. We needed to make this visit short.

I looked around the yard and into the forest just beyond, hoping to spot something. I didn't have to wait long. Sean's form materialized, and he strode in my direction, pointing his finger at me.

"You. I want to talk to you."

I let out a little gasp, surprised by his intensity, and Zane put a protective arm around my shoulders.

"What's going on?" he asked, scanning the area.

"Sean's ghost just appeared. It's okay. He seems a little upset. It's expected," I said, trying to smile as I turned to face the specter. "Hi Sean, do you remember me from yesterday?"

"Yes, and I want to know what's going on," Sean said. "Why are you the only one who can see me? There was a lady up here and she acted like I'm invisible. I demand to know what kind of game is going on here?"

"Who's been up here?" I asked.

"Some woman, I don't know who she is. She was dressed like a cleaning lady. She was here a little while ago. I followed her into the house through the door, but she ignored me completely. What is going on?"

He punctuated his last question with a stabbing finger that went right through my shoulder. I flinched a little at the feeling of cold and Zane tightened his grip.

"What's he saying?"

I quickly summed it up for Zane while Sean listened with his head cocked.

"Why can't he hear me? Why are you repeating what I said?"

"Sean, I don't know how else to tell you this, but you passed away.

We're trying to figure out how you were killed. Do you have any memories of what happened?"

He shook his head furiously, pacing back and forth.

"I'm not dead. I can't be dead. I have so much to do."

"You know how you just tried to poke my shoulder? Did you see your finger go through it?"

"That means nothing."

"Okay... try touching the railing on the deck. Grab on to it."

Sometimes, realizing they were no longer corporal, drove home the truth to a new ghost, but Sean really seemed resistant to accepting his death. I guess I couldn't blame him after seeing his body.

He walked over to the deck and stared at me triumphantly for a second as he tried to grab the deck. His face fell as his hand went right through the wood.

"No. No, no, no. This can't be happening. I'm still in a weird dream somehow and none of this is real."

I stepped out of Zane's comforting embrace and approached Sean slowly.

"I'm so sorry. I can help you pass on, if you're ready."

"Pass on? I'm not ready to pass on. I'm ready to go home and get back to my life. I must have eaten some rotten food."

He kept muttering and trying to grab the railing, failing each time. Zane walked closer, and I told him what I was seeing. He shook his head.

"Does this happen a lot?"

"Sometimes, especially if a death was violent. It can take time to accept their new reality."

"I'm right here, you know. What do you mean by violent death?"

I swallowed hard and laid it all out for him. Everything I'd seen and what his friends said. He looked so lost I ached to comfort him somehow.

"All I know is that you can move on. There's a much better place out there. I've seen glimpses of it. I'd like to help you."

"You can help me by figuring out who or what killed me. You were saying something about a wild animal? Oh my God, is Violet okay? She didn't get hurt, too, did she?"

"Violet? I thought you were dating Trish?" I asked, suspicion rearing its head in the back of my mind.

He looked at me, blanking his expression.

"Right, Trish. Her too. Sorry, I just had a flash of a memory of talking to Violet before it all goes black. She'd been going through a lot lately, and we'd been talking a lot."

I filed away my suspicion for later.

"They're all fine. It's super common to have flashes of memory right after you've been, well, separated from your body. More details should start coming back to you."

He looked at me and I noticed he was fading around the edges. We had little time. I felt a few drops of rain on my forehead and looked up at the sky. Yeah, I needed to wrap this up.

"Do you know of anyone who would've wanted to kill you? I don't think it was a wild animal. Did anyone you were staying with have a grudge against you?"

He shook his head, looking mournful as he faded further.

"No, we were all pretty tight. Trevor can be a jerk, but that's just his way. I can't believe it. I'll never see them again, will I?"

"You will, I'm sure of it. When the time is right. Do you have any message you want to pass on?"

He wavered, becoming more transparent. As he faded out completely, I heard him whisper.

"Tell Violet..."

He vanished, and I looked around, frustrated.

"Tell Violet what?" I said, shouting even though I knew it wouldn't do any good.

Zane looked at me with his forehead furrowed.

"What did he say?"

I motioned for Zane to follow me and led him back inside the cabin, away from the rain that was coming down, as I relayed what Sean said.

"Do you think he was having an affair with Violet?" Zane asked.

"It's possible, I guess. It's weird that she was the first person he thought of. He tried to brush it off, but I could tell by the tone of his voice he was really worried about her."

"That gives us a few people with motives, then."

I raised my hand and ticked off their names on my fingers.

"Trevor, if he found out his best friend was bonking his girlfriend. Trish, who was hoping for a proposal and maybe even Violet if she found out he wouldn't leave Trish."

"Bonking?" Zane asked, a smile quirking his lips.

I blushed and looked away.

"You know what I mean."

He put his arm around me and pulled me close, ruffling my hair gently.

"What do we do now, boss?"

My lips quirked at that.

"Well, I think we should get back down the hill before the rain gets worse. I was hoping to talk to Ned, but I don't want to wait too long."

"Okay, let's lock up and we'll head home. Do you have anything else to do today?"

"I need to stop by the hotel and get those rooms ready for painting. Did you want to come with me or do you need to check in with your client?"

"I need to follow-up with a few things, but I'll go with you to the hotel and then take you home."

We stepped outside and paused under the covered porch. The rain was beating down on the metal roof, making it sound much worse than it was. Zane made a break for it, but I stopped when I saw something out of the corner of my eye.

There, in the trees, was a familiar figure. I waved to Zane who'd already made it into his Jeep, and walked to the side of the porch, trying to stay under the overhang. I tried to see through the wind-swept rain and almost jumped out of my skin when a voice sounded right behind me.

"Lookin' for someone?"

"Geez, you scared me," I said, whipping around and spotting Ned. "Is that a bear skin rug?"

Now that he was close, I could finally make out his shape. He was a short man and must have suffered a back injury when he was alive. He was bent almost double and his eyes peered out from inside the rug. It was a weird quirk of the afterlife that ghosts usually appeared in the last clothes they were wearing. I didn't understand it, and one of these days, I was going to ask Charles Thurgood about it. He'd been a ghost for almost as long as Ned.

"Shore is. This cost me a pretty penny. I'm just glad when I passed I was wearing it. I would've missed it."

"I thought you were some sort of strange bear-like creature the first time I saw you. That explains everything."

He let out a wheezing laugh and slapped his knee that echoed around the porch. I couldn't believe it made an actual noise.

"How do you do that?"

"Do what?"

"How do you move things and make sounds? Most ghosts can't do that."

"Now I think that's for me to know and you to find out. Can't go revealing all my secrets, can I?"

"You're really Edward Davis?"

"Like I said before, girly, they called me Ned. Edward is too stuffy for a fella like me."

"Why are you appearing here and scaring people? You had nothing to do with that man's death, did you?"

He straightened up a little and spit to the side. I half expected to see real spit, but thankfully, he apparently wasn't capable of conjuring that.

"I didn't do nothing wrong, you take that back. Might have seen something, but I don't think I'll tell you now. Don't appreciate being accused of something I didn't do."

I reached a hand out, half expecting to feel the rough, greasy fur of the rug. It didn't look all that clean, and I was thankful it wasn't corporal.

"I'm sorry. I wasn't trying to imply that. What did you see?"

"Mebbe I'll tell you. Mebbe not."

He gave a cackling laugh and disappeared. A flower pot fell over next to me and I felt a powerful gust of air blow past. Darn it. I really blew that. I made a dash for Zane's Jeep and dove inside, shaking off the rain.

"Was that Ned?" Zane asked, digging in the backseat for something.

He handed me a dry tee-shirt, and I used it to towel off my wet hair while nodding.

"Yep, that was him. I made him mad though."

Zane backed down the drive as I told him what Ned had to say. He shook his head and focused on the road as we slowly made our way back down the mountain.

"It's never dull, that's for sure. To the hotel?"

I let out a sigh, feeling like a bedraggled poodle, although I'm sure I looked more like a drowned rat. I resisted the urge to look at myself in the visor mirror. I didn't need to see.

"Yeah, let's head that way."

I watched the rain come down in sheets as we drove. Zane was a skilled driver, and I felt at ease as he navigated the hairpin turns like they were straightaways. I thought about everything we'd learned and tried to make sense of it before giving up. I was missing an important piece of the puzzle, but I was determined to find it.

11

By the time we made it to the hotel, the rain was tapering off, and a beautiful double rainbow was just visible over the hills. I stopped on the sidewalk and admired it for a second before following Zane inside. The lobby of the hotel was busier than normal, and I spotted Kelsie running back and forth, looking harried. I gave her a little wave as Zane and I stepped into the elevator. The doors slid shut, and the noise faded as we headed to the fourth floor.

"Geez, that was crazy," Zane said. "I wonder what's going on?"

"I'm not sure, but poor Kelsie looked like she was at her wit's end, there."

The door creaked open, and we stepped into the hall. The rhythmic sound of sanding led us down the corridor towards the room at the end of the hall. I peeked in and saw one of Logan's workers, Tim, working on smoothing the seam on the sheetrock.

"Hey, Tim. How's it going?" I asked.

He stopped and wiped the dust from his face. Sanding sheetrock was one of my least favorite jobs, and I was thrilled Logan's crew had come back to work once I'd helped the banshee pass on. I'd been helping him with the demo of the rooms, but this was a task I preferred to avoid.

"He should be down at the other end, crossing off his checklist. Hopefully, we're all good."

I let him get back to work and joined Zane in the hall. He had his phone up to his ear, so I pointed out where I was going. He followed behind me, preoccupied with whoever he was talking to. I noticed a door propped open and stuck my head inside, spotting Logan with his clipboard, wearing a deep frown.

"Hey, why so serious?" I asked as I walked into the room.

"Freckles. Long time, no see. I'm just focused on making sure we've gotten everything done," Logan said before giving me a quick hug. "Where's your hunk of burning love?"

I made a face and stepped back, looking around the room.

"Let's not make that nickname a thing, okay? He's out in the hall on the phone. This looks amazing."

I checked out the changes he'd made in the room and nodded my approval. Everything was shaping up and, like he'd said, I'd be ready to get the painters going with the colors I'd chosen for the new suites. Since the hotel was built in the early 1900s, I was going with a color scheme from that time period and I couldn't wait to see how it was all going to turn out.

"Thanks. It feels good to be getting closer to finishing up our end of the work. We've got about six jobs lined up after this, so I'd like to get it done as fast as we can. What time is it?"

I slid my phone out of my pocket and glanced at the screen.

"Right before lunch."

"Sweet, I'm starving. Do you and Lover Boy want to eat with me?"

"Ew, that's an even worse nickname, and that's saying something. Let's just go with Zane, okay?"

"Go with Zane where?" he asked from the doorway. "Hey, Logan."

"Hey, man. Just teasing this one," Logan said, ruffling my hair.

I rolled my eyes and stepped around Logan, intentionally bumping him with my shoulder. He rubbed his shoulder and followed me.

"Do you want to have lunch with Logan and Kelsie? If she can get away, that is."

Zane nodded and Logan hurried to catch up with me as we walked into the hall.

"What's up with Kelsie?"

"There was a bunch of people in the lobby and she looked super busy."

Logan nodded and walked ahead, heading for the room where Tim was working.

"Let me tell Tim it's lunch time and then we can head downstairs."

I turned back to Zane and smiled at him. He looked a little preoccupied as he punched the button for the elevator.

"Was everything okay on your call?" I asked.

"I've got to run down to Creekside after lunch. That new client isn't happy that we have caught no one with the cameras I installed. He's insisting they're not working."

"Oh man, that stinks. I'm sure whoever's been stealing stuff is waiting to make their move."

"Hopefully, I can convince him of that. I'll have to do a check of the equipment."

The doors opened, and we stepped in. I poked my head back out and stuck my tongue out at Logan as he jogged our way.

"Hurry, slow poke. I'm starving," I said.

"Whatever, Copper Top," he said, poking my side as he joined us in the elevator. "You're the slow one, I'm the handsome one."

Zane snorted as the doors closed and we headed down to the lobby. Logan gave me a cheeky grin, and I glared at him before poking him in the chest.

"Zip it. No one needs another nickname right now."

His eyes twinkled, and I shook my head, grateful that the doors to the elevator opened before his mouth could. The lobby was a lot quieter and Kelsie was leaning against the desk, looking like she needed a break. Logan's smile deepened and my inner matchmaker gave a little cheer and a hop as he walked towards her. There was definitely a connection between these two. Zane put an arm around my waist and pulled me close.

"Just let it happen at their own pace," he said, smiling down at me.

"Hey, I don't meddle. Much. Okay, maybe a little. They look so cute together, though," I said, watching Kelsie's face light up as Logan walked up to her.

We joined the couple, and I didn't miss the way Logan's face had softened as he leaned close to Kelsie to say something meant only for her ears. Her eyes shone as she looked back at him and nodded.

"Hey, Kelsie. It looks like everyone cleared out," I said.

She smiled at me and let out a sigh.

"Finally. That was just a disaster. Do you guys mind if we have lunch here? I want to stay close in case we have some more late check-outs."

"What happened?" Logan asked as we fell in together and walked towards the hotel restaurant.

"We've got a new girl delivering the check-out invoices, and she put the wrong ones under the wrong doors. People were flipping out, thinking they were being overcharged."

"Oh no, that doesn't sound like much fun to sort out," I said, sliding into a booth and grabbing a menu off the middle of the table.

"It wasn't," she said as she sat next to me.

Logan and Zane sat across from us and Zane reached across the table to grab my hand. Logan's eyebrows quirked, and I pointed at him.

"Nope, not that one, either," I said, figuring he was coming up with yet another corny nickname for Zane.

He mock-pouted before turning his attention to his own menu. Kelsie shook her head and smiled over at me.

"I love how you two act more like siblings than cousins."

"You say that now, but give it a few months," I said, rolling my eyes. "I'm sure that feeling will wear off."

Logan slapped his hand over his heart and gasped.

"I'm wounded you would say that, Brynnie."

"Yeah, yeah," I said, flapping my hand in his direction. "Kelsie, is the French Dip pretty good here?"

She nodded enthusiastically.

"It's amazing. That's one of my favorites."

"That's settled for me, then. What are you having, Zane?"

Zane looked back at his menu.

"I'm thinking of a bacon cheeseburger with onion rings."

"Oh, don't do that," Logan said, smirking. "You won't be able to smoochie smooch with Brynn afterwards."

"I'll get them, too," I said, sticking my tongue out at Logan. "Why don't you worry about your own breath? I'm sure Kelsie would appreciate that."

Kelsie blushed and fiddled with the edge of her menu.

"It's okay, onions don't bother me."

Our server came up and took our orders, and I couldn't help but notice Logan went with regular fries. I raised my eyebrow at him after he ordered and he blushed a little, too. They were so cute together. I never thought I'd see my cousin, well-known for being a love them and leave them type, blushing over a girl. Score!

The server returned with our drinks and I busied myself getting my straw unwrapped, determined not to tease him anymore in front of Kelsie.

"So, what's been happening with your case?" Kelsie asked. "Logan said something about a cabin up at the ski resort?"

I nodded, grateful that Kelsie was well aware of my abilities, and while I knew it wasn't easy for her to accept what I did, she was open-minded and didn't tease me about it anymore. We'd come a long way since high school.

"We ran into some interesting people today," I said, launching into a recap of our morning.

Zane filled in some details I'd missed as Kelsie and Logan listened raptly. Kelsie's brow furrowed, and she glanced over at me.

"It sounds like Sean was running around on Trish with Violet, don't you think? Is it possible she's the one who killed him?"

I shook my head, spotting our server returning with our order. I slid my drink to the side.

"I'm not sure. The thing that's throwing me off is how he was killed. I won't go into it before we eat, but I don't think Trish would've been capable of something like that."

Kelsie shuddered while Logan grimaced.

"Yeah, let's not talk about that right now," he said as the server put our plates in front of us.

We focused on our food for the next few minutes, munching away happily. The sandwich was just as good as Kelsie said it would be, and I appreciated the tang of the onion rings with the savory beef. I was almost finished with my meal when my phone rang. I wiped my mouth and answered the call.

"Hi, Brynn. We just got the results back from the coroner. It's a little surprising," Dave said, his voice sounding puzzled. "I thought you might want to know since you were going to interview the room-mates this morning."

"We left from there a little while ago. What do you mean?" I asked, dredging my last onion ring through some ketchup.

"He was poisoned."

Dave's gruff, matter-of-fact statement caught me off guard. I dropped the onion ring and focused on what he was saying, sure I'd heard him wrong.

"Poisoned? But..."

My mind raced as I thought back to how Sean's body looked at the scene that morning. It just made little sense.

"All that damage was done after he was already dead."

My lunch threatened to make a reappearance, and I swallowed hard, completely uninterested in grabbing that last onion ring again.

"This changes everything."

"Yeah. We never were one hundred percent sure it was a wild animal attack, but now this is definitely an active murder investiga-tion. Do you have a minute to stop by my office? I'd like to hear what you found out this morning."

"Sure, I can be there in half an hour."

I ended the call and looked across the table at Zane. He was frowning as he finished up the last of his lunch.

"What did Dave have to say?"

I shook my head, not wanting to bring Logan and Kelsie in on the gory details.

"Just that the cause of death was not what was expected."

He nodded, understanding me instantly. I wiped my hands and took a last sip of my Coke before glancing over at Logan. His look told me he wanted to know what was going on, but he didn't want to ask in front of Kelsie. I shook my head slightly.

"I probably don't want to know, huh?" Kelsie asked, giving me a wry smile.

"Yeah, no. Not after lunch, anyway. I need to go talk to Dave."

She shook her head and slid her plate away.

"You get involved in the most interesting cases, Brynn."

I smiled wryly as we all got up to leave.

"It's a gift, I guess."

Logan surprised me by paying for everyone's lunch after we walked up to the register. He ruffled my hair again before pulling me in for a quick hug.

"My treat. I didn't get to buy you guys dinner the other night."

We headed back into the lobby and stopped in front of the elevators.

"Thanks, Logan. I'll get the painters scheduled and make sure they have the right colors. Do you think they can start tomorrow?"

"Sure, we should be done by the end of the day. After that's done, we can figure out the logistics of getting the furniture delivered."

"I'll definitely want to be here for that. Thanks for lunch."

Zane and I left Logan and Kelsie in the lobby and headed back outside. The gloomy weather had fled, leaving blue skies and bright sunshine in its wake. Once we were back in Zane's Jeep, he turned to me.

"What did Dave have to say?"

I explained the coroner's results and Zane shook his head as he steered towards my place so I could get my car.

"I guess on the upside, poor Sean wasn't mauled to death. But that's pretty cold to poison someone and then maul the body," I said.

"That shows either some premeditation or some desperate

thinking to cover their tracks. Which one do you think could've done it?"

"This really throws a kink in what I was thinking. Could one person have done all of that damage? You didn't see the body, but it was bad,"

I grimaced as the vision of Sean's body flashed through my head again. We were dealing with a sick person, that was for sure. Zane looked over at me as we pulled to a stop in front of my house.

"I don't like it, Brynn. Promise me you won't go back up there alone. Now that Dave's signed off on me being a consultant, I want to go with you if you interview anyone else or go back up there."

"I appreciate that. I'll be careful. Now, I'd like to remind you I also had onion rings for lunch..." I said, grinning over at him.

Zane's lips quirked in a smile as he leaned across the seat.

"That's right. You did. What a lovely coincidence. I guess you won't mind if I do this?"

His kiss started out soft but deepened, surprising me with his intensity. I lost track of all time and space before he pulled back, breathing hard.

"Wow," I said.

"Wow is right. Where am I?"

He smoothed my hair and kissed me again, softly this time. I smiled at him as we rested our foreheads together.

"I'll call you later," I said, opening up the door of the Jeep.

"See you, Sullivan."

"Later, Matthews."

I floated into the house and promptly tripped over Bernie, who was staring at me with a belligerent look on his little face.

"Sorry! I always do that."

He continued to bore a hole through my head as he stared at me.

"Okay, okay, you can come with me to see Dave. Kennel up."

He stalked into his bag, tail head high, and turned around majestically, folding his paws.

I grabbed his bag and my keys before heading back outside. I couldn't wait to see what Dave had to say about this case. Things were getting stranger by the minute.

12

I kept Bernie entertained by telling him about my visit up to the cabins and what I'd run into. He chirped when I told him about the coroner's report and looked over at me. I nodded and focused back on the road.

"I know, bud. It just seems weird. His body was in such terrible shape, I never would have thought it would be poison."

Bernie stretched, standing on his tiptoes in the front seat as I found a place to park by the Sheriff's office. He hopped into his bag and turned around, staring at me.

"Of course I'll take you in with me. I wouldn't dream of leaving you behind, your highness."

He huffed, and I shook my head as I climbed out of the car and put the strap of his bag over my shoulder. Once again, I wished we could talk like we did in the in-between. This whole crime saving thing would probably be a lot easier if he could speak. He had an uncanny way of seeming to know all the answers.

Since that didn't seem to be a possibility, I was just going to do the legwork and hope I got lucky. Bernie meowed softly as I walked up the steps, and I assumed that meant he felt the same way. I waved at the officer sitting at the front desk and walked back to Dave's office. He was kicked back in his chair, per usual, with his feet propped up on the desk and his cowboy hat perched on the back of his head.

"Don't put your feet down on my account," I said as I walked in and flopped into the chair across from his desk.

"I won't. Thanks for coming over, I realize I probably interrupted your lunch."

I flapped a hand at him before situating Bernie's bag at my feet.

"We were almost done. Thanks for making Zane a consultant, by the way. It meant a lot to him."

"I figured I needed to keep you safe. You seem to keep running into issues. This way he can watch over you when I can't."

I thought about rolling my eyes, but he had a point. The past several weeks I'd ended up at the mercy of a crazed would-be serial killer, and a creep with a serious Oedipus complex. I settled for a smile instead.

"You said you wanted to know about my interviews this morning with Sean's friends?"

"Absolutely. Hit me."

I took him through my interviews and paused for a second. Ever since we'd worked together when I was in high school, Dave had known about my ability to speak with ghosts. That didn't mean he was entirely comfortable with it. He seemed to sense my hesitation and leaned forward onto his desk.

"Spit it out, I can tell you have more to say."

I described how Sean's ghost was not accepting his passing and how'd mentioned Violet instead of Trish when I'd broken the news to him.

"And then, I saw the ghost of the bear creature and talked to him. He says he saw something, but I irritated him and he disappeared. I'm hoping the next time I see him I'll get him to talk."

"Wait, what?" Dave asked, leaning back so fast his cowboy hat fell off the back of his head.

I suppressed a giggle at his facial expression.

"Sorry, I guess I forgot to tell you the most important part first. The bear creature isn't a bear at all. The best I can tell, he's the ghost of an old miner, named Edward Davis. He's got some sort of back issue, and he was killed while he was wearing a bear skin rug. Ghosts usually appear clothed in what they were last wearing. It's strange though..." I said, trailing off.

"Okay, after listening to that, I'm wondering what on earth you think is strange?"

"It's just that he's capable of making noise and moving things. Like actually physically manipulating his environment. I've seen nothing like it before."

Dave rescued his cowboy hat and crammed it back on his head. He looked thoroughly confused, and I couldn't blame him. I wasn't sure I understood it all, either.

"I'm out of my depth here, so I'm going to let you worry about that side of things. From what I can gather, we're dealing with a poisoner in this case. I don't know how the body was mauled after the fact, but that's what the coroner said."

I blanched a little at his wording.

"How does he even know that?"

"Something about blood coagulation and some other big words I hardly understood. Paul's a good man, and he's good at his job. If that's what he says, that's what happened. I will say I noticed there wasn't much blood on the grass given the state of his body. I guess it all makes sense."

I swallowed hard and Bernie let out a loud meow, startling me and Tom. He chuckled and leaned back in his chair again.

"I see you brought your cat with you again."

"He likes to come with. Sometimes I think he's a better sleuth than I am."

Bernie let out another meow, making me laugh before I continued.

"Sorry, he's a much better sleuth. So, what do we do now? Did Paul say what the poison was?"

"Oleander."

"Really? That's an odd one. Wasn't there a movie about something like that?" I asked.

"Not sure. The only thing I am sure about is this was a murder, and it was most likely done by a woman. The poisoning, anyway. I'm not sure who damaged the body after the fact."

"Why a woman? Is that the old saying that a poison is a woman's weapon?" I asked, bristling a little.

"Put your hackles down. I didn't say it. But the science proves that typically, when poison is involved, a woman did it."

"Or a man used it to frame a woman."

"Point taken. Anyway, since Treadwell wasn't from here, that leads straight to the people who knew him best. I'm gonna have to go up and question those kids again."

"Let me know if you want me to come with you."

He shook his head and stood up from his desk. I grabbed Bernie's bag and followed him out of the office.

"I think we'll let them think we're working separately. It sounds like you got way out of them than I did. Maybe when I'm done, you can circle back and see what they say."

"Devious," I said, grinning at him. "I like it."

He tipped his hat and walked towards the back while I headed back outside. I knew little about poisons or plants. Paints, wallpaper and wood stain were more my thing. But I knew someone who did, or at least someone with access to that information.

"Bernie, you ready to go see Sophie again?"

He chirped, which I took to mean heck yes, mom, let's go. I got in my car and drove the short distance to the library. As I walked in, I looked around for the new girl but didn't see her. Jingling bracelets foretold Sophie's appearance, and I smiled as she rounded the corner, arms open wide.

"Brynn! Just who I was hoping to see. I was going to call you. Divine providence!"

"What's up?"

Sophie peeked around my shoulder and waved at Bernie, who

meowed softly. She held her finger up to her lips and motioned for me to follow. I fell in behind the wake created by her flowing skirts and nearly had to trot to keep up.

"I found something interesting about Edward Davis. I've got it ready for you in the Dakota Room."

"Really?" I asked, struggling not to gasp for breath as I hustled behind her.

I really needed to work out more.

"Yes, I think you'll find it most useful. Do you have any updates for me, dear?"

"Actually, I do. You'll never guess what's happened over the past few days."

She pulled a chair out for me once we'd reached the research room and I sank into it gratefully, pausing for a second before bringing her up to speed on everything that had happened over the past two days. Her hand crept up to her chest as I described the crime scene, carefully omitting the gory parts. When I got to the part about the poison, she cocked her head to the side.

"Oleander? That's strange."

"Why? I know nothing about it."

"Well, it doesn't grow here. It gets way too cold for it to grow in the wild. If it is grown, it has to be cultivated and kept inside during the winter. It's such a toxic plant, even touching it can make you sick. It can't be used even in compost."

"Fascinating. I didn't know. It's that bad?"

"Terrible, darling. I'll pull some research material for you on that, while you read what I found."

She slid a book over to me and patted me on the shoulder as she hustled out of the room. I turned the book over to look at the spine. The title read *Mining Wars in the South Dakota Gold Rush*. I opened the book and quickly got lost, reliving the feuds that broke out between small time miners and the big companies who wanted their claims. I almost forgot I was reading for a purpose and quickly started paging through, looking for something that applied to Ned. My eyes lit up when I came to a chapter that described the ski resort area where the cabin was now and I started reading.

Sophie came back into the room, bracelets jingling merrily. I couldn't help but smile at the conundrum she presented. A librarian, the so-called guardian of silence, who made that much noise. I wouldn't change her for the world.

"Sophie, it says here that Edward Davis was believed to have been killed by Herbert Mason, following the dispute of a claim, but it was never proven. I wonder if he was killed on the grounds near the cabin and that's why he appears there?"

"You've contacted him then?"

I told her about my experience dealing with Ned's ghost and her eyes shone with wonder as I described his ability to manipulate his environment.

"I've talked to Sean Treadwell, the victim, too, but not since I discovered how he was killed. I need to get back up there and see if I can find him again. I'm worried about him. Normally, a ghost will accept their new reality, but he seems to struggle. I just wish I could help him."

I went quiet as I thought about all the strange facets of this case. A murdered miner from over a century ago. A property owned by the descendant of the man who reportedly killed him. A dead man who's friends swear they heard nothing and blamed a wild animal. I had a feeling nearly everyone was lying to me and I wasn't sure how to find the truth. Bernie rustled in his bag and meowed sadly. I reached up to the mesh and rubbed his side.

"This is certainly a dastardly, deceitful..." Sophie said, pausing for me to complete her sentence in the little game we always played.

I paused for a second and then smiled.

"Debacle."

"Excellent! You'll figure it out, dear, you always do. I need to get back up front. Would you like to take these books home?" she asked, nodding to the book on poisonous plants she'd brought with her.

"Yes, please. Where's Stacia?"

"I've got her going through the archives today to learn what's back there."

I gathered up Bernie's bag while Sophie took the books and followed her to the front desk. I needed answers, and I wasn't sure how to get them. I thanked Sophie for the books and headed back into the waning sunshine. It had been a long day, and I was ready to head home and try to put my jumbled thoughts in order.

13

Once I was back home, I spread out the books I'd borrowed on the kitchen table and gathered up all my notes. Bernie hopped on the table and laid down smack in the middle of my notebook and blinked at me slowly.

"What? I know, Bernie. There are way too many open threads in this case and it's hard to know where to start."

He kneaded the notebook edge with his paws, clicking the spiral binding with his sharp claws. Note to self, clip his nails later. He was carrying around some serious weapons. I took the hint and sat down, gently moving him to the side so I could open up my notes. I read through everything and turned to a fresh sheet, ready to start a new list.

A familiar engine cut off outside and Bernie jumped down, jogging towards the front door. I followed him and opened the door to see Zane standing there, laden with takeout bags. Now, this was my idea of a glorious thing.

"I hope you don't mind me dropping by. I figured you were buried in this case and would forget to eat if I didn't," Zane said as I let him in.

I followed him, entranced by the smell coming from the bags.

"What is that delicious smell?" I asked, taking another sniff.

"A new Greek restaurant opened in Creekside. I was driving by and couldn't resist. I figured you'd like it."

"I'm pretty sure I"m going to love it. I'll clean off the table."

I hurried over to the table and stacked the books and my notes to the side before helping Zane get the food transferred to plates. Bernie wound around my ankles, meowing piteously, as if it had been years since he'd last eaten. Honestly, my stomach must have felt the same way from the growling noises it was producing.

"Do you want the chicken or beef gyro?" Zane asked.

I thought for a second and went back to the kitchen for a knife.

"Let's split them and see which one is best."

"I like the way you think."

Zane gave me a quick kiss on the cheek before divvying up the gyros and swapping out two halves. The fries smelled amazing and I couldn't wait to dip them in the cucumber sauce. Bernie joined us on the table, making Zane chuckle. He ripped off a tiny piece of chicken and handed it over to my greedy little beast, who snapped it up and swallowed it whole.

"Well, it certainly has Bernie's seal of approval," I said, digging into the chicken gyro.

The next few minutes passed in silence as we made quick work of our meal. I declared it a tie between the chicken and beef and started at the baklava, wondering if I had any room left.

"It's tiny, Brynn. Have a piece," Zane said, slicing off a section and putting it on my plate.

I took a bite and my eyes closed in pure bliss.

"Wow. Just wow. I don't know when I've ever had food this good. I'm so glad you stopped by. And it's good to see you, of course."

I winked at him as I gathered up the plates and headed back to the kitchen. Zane helped get everything cleaned up while Bernie weaved between our legs, hoping for just one more treat. I wiped down the counter and looked over at Zane.

"How did the rest of your day go? Is your client still upset?"

"No, I think I got him talked down off the ledge. He was expecting instant results, but once he saw the equipment was all working as it should, he calmed down. It's a waiting game."

"That's good. I learned a few interesting things from Dave. I was just sitting down to list everything out and try to make sense of it."

"Want to run it by me?"

We sat at the table and I spread the books back out and grabbed my notebook.

"Okay, so we know the following things. First, the land where the cabin now sits was owned by Edward Davis. He got into a feud with Herbert Mason, who eventually ended up winning the claim and taking the land. Shortly after, Davis died, and a bear-like creature was spotted a few years later. After that, it wasn't reported for nearly a hundred years until a few months ago."

"I'm following you so far. Isn't the new owner's name Mason as well?"

I nodded and chewed on my pen, thoughts running around like headless chickens.

"It is. He claimed not to know if there was a connection, but I think he was lying."

"So, we need to research and find out if there is indeed a link between the original Mason and the new owner and what happened to the property in between the periods when they owned it."

"Excellent, I'll mark that down. I've got the abstract printed out. It should be on the table in the living room."

He jumped up to grab the file while I went over the next few points in my head. Zane returned, and I continued down my list.

"Next, we know that the renters at the cabin started leaving critical reviews about three months ago and mentioned seeing the creature. Trent Mason bought the place a few months before that. We've confirmed that the so-called ghost bear is in fact the ghost of the dead miner, Edward Davis, or Ned, as he prefers to be called."

Zane shook his head and let out a laugh.

"Well, I like Ned a lot better than a ghost bear."

"Me too. He has abilities I've never seen in a ghost before, and honestly, until I found out the cause of death was poison, I had a stray thought he might have been capable of murder. If he can move things, he could conceivably hurt someone. It was a slight chance, but I think we can cross him off the suspect list for the new murder."

"What did you find out about the poison?"

I told Zane what I'd learned about Oleander from Dave and Sophie. He nodded thoughtfully and picked up the book, paging through it while I talked.

"Dave says women are usually the ones who are behind poisonings, but I'm having a hard time wrapping my head around a woman intentionally mauling a dead body. That just seems too hideous to contemplate."

"It's pretty hideous for a man to do that, too."

"True. Okay, so point three. We have a group of friends who rented the cabin where the ghost was seen. One of them ends up dead. He may or may not have been having an affair with his best friend's girlfriend. We've got maybe three concrete suspects with them. Dave's pretty sure it had to have been one of them since Sean Treadwell wasn't from here."

"That makes sense. So, how do you think it all ties together?"

I threw my hands up in the air and shrugged.

"Heck if I know. I wouldn't be involved with the case at all if it wasn't for Ned's ghost. I'm not sure there is any connection at all. Maybe I'm letting the murder case take me away from my primary goal here, but I'm so invested in the story, I can't let it go and just focus on the ghost."

Bernie jumped on the table and sat next to Zane, looking between us. I raised my eyebrow at him and he huffed a sigh before clawing at the book next to Zane.

"Does he do this often?" Zane asked.

"He does. In fact, he's the one who finds most of the clues."

Zane stroked Bernie's head before opening the book again and looking for the index. He read for a few minutes while I continued making notes and creating a list of steps I needed to take next. Zane let out a sharp breath, and I looked up.

"It says here that oleander can be used in witchcraft, and it may even be tied to a ritual sacrifice."

"Really? Do you think any of the girls we talked to today were witches?"

He shrugged and continued reading.

"I guess it's possible. Are there actual witches in these times? I didn't know that was a thing."

"Well, there are wiccans around here in the Hills. I think most of them are good-hearted people who wouldn't hurt a fly. Oleander seems like a deadly herb. I mean, even the leaves are deadly, so growing it would be a concerted effort, especially in this state. I guess it's possible we're dealing with someone who may dabble in the craft."

He closed the book and scratched Bernie's head again. He leaned against Zane's broad shoulder and closed his eyes. I feel the same way, cat. I went back to my list and made a few finishing touches.

"What's the plan?" Zane asked, leaning over the table to peek at it.

"I need to track down the line of ownership for the cabin. Maybe I can find some genealogy stuff online that will help me link Trent to Herbert Mason. Next, I need to talk to Ned again, if he'll answer my questions. He said he'd seen something, but he clammed up and disappeared. I need to know what he saw."

"And we need to figure out if any of the people who rented that cabin are capable of murder."

"Exactly."

"Tell you what, you focus on the cabin haunting and I'll see what I can find out about Treadwell's friends. I've got access to some pretty powerful background check apps."

"That would be amazing. I enjoy working with you, Matthews. You're useful."

"That's not all I can do," Zane said with a wink.

"Really? Is there no end to your talents?"

"I like to think I'm pretty well-rounded. Although after that meal, I should say I'm just round," he said, patting his flat stomach.

I rolled my eyes and packed up my notes, feeling like I finally had a plan. Bernie thumped down from the table and stretched as he made his way to his favorite spot on the couch.

"Want to watch a movie?" I asked.

I wasn't sure I was ready for what he was insinuating, but I wouldn't turn down a pleasant night with him, watching a movie and getting to know each other better. I glanced over at him, hoping he understood my feelings. He smiled, eyes crinkling, and walked around the table before gently pulling me into a warm hug.

"There's nothing I'd like more."

We joined Bernie on the couch and I clicked through my DVR listing before picking The Avengers. It was probably the twentieth time I'd seen it, so my mind was free to wander through the tangled forest of my thoughts as I nestled next to Zane. It was nice to have a partner in crime. Bernie glanced up at me and let out a cranky meow. Whoops. A second partner in crime. No one could replace my special cat, but it was nice having a security expert who knew how to pull people's backgrounds.

I rubbed behind Bernie's ears and he relaxed next to me, purring happily. I closed the mental door to my thoughts and relaxed, determined to enjoy this evening. Tomorrow, I would double down and see what I could learn from Ned. This time, I'd bring Bernie with me. No one could resist him, even ghosts, and he made an excellent bridge for communicating with spirits. I leaned my head on Zane's shoulder and he put an arm around me, pulling me close. A handsome, thoughtful man who delivered Greek food while offering to help me solve a case, and a faithful cat. You really can't get much better than that.

14

The next morning, I found myself full of hope and feeling much lighter than I had the previous day. It might have been the sun shining through my windshield, the blue sky peeking through the tips of the trees, or that I'd hung out with Zane, but I loving this feeling. Bernie shifted positions on his seat as we headed up the mountain and I reached over to ruffle his fur. His brilliant green eyes met mine and I'm pretty sure he was smiling, too.

"Think we'll be able to find some ghosts today, Bernie? I'd love to find some answers, too, while we're at it."

He gave the kitty equivalent of a shrug and looked back out the window. I wondered what he thought of the terrain as we climbed past the mine. I ignored the ugly, open-cut scar on the mountain when I went this way, but I suppose it had its purpose. People had relied on gold from these hills for decades. As I drove up the last stretch of road to the cabin, I wondered what Herbert Mason was like. Was he a nice man, or was he ruthless?

I parked my car and loaded Bernie into his bag before walking around to the back of the cabin. There was a feeling of crispness in the air that said fall was right around the corner, but the bright sunshine swiftly warmed it away as I sat on the back deck. I waited patiently, debating on whether to release Bernie from his carrier. I trusted my cat, but I knew he could be a target of a much larger animal in the woods. We may not have bears, but there were certainly mountain lions around, and I didn't want Bernie to end up as a snack for one of them.

He meowed from his bag and I looked around before grabbing the zipper.

"Fine, but promise me you'll avoid the trees. Stay where I can see you at all times, okay?"

He shot me a look that summed up his feelings on my lecture, and I'm pretty sure he rolled his eyes at me before stalking around the deck, sniffing the air. His fur ruffled, and I felt a chill sneak around the edges of my shirt sleeves. I looked straight ahead and smiled when I saw Sean Treadwell's form appear in front of me.

He looked much more resigned than he had the past few times I'd seen him and my heart went out to him.

"Hi Sean, is everything okay?"

He snorted and looked around at his nearly translucent form before making eye contact.

"You mean besides the fact that I'm dead?"

I winced. He had a good point. Still, it encouraged me he seemed to accept his fate and seemed more at peace with everything.

"I'm sorry. I wasn't trying to be thoughtless. I learned something interesting about your, um, passing, yesterday."

He drifted closer.

"Yes? Do you know who killed me?"

"Not yet, but I know how you died. It wasn't a wild animal. You were poisoned with oleander."

"Ole-what?"

"It's a type of shrubby thing, I guess. It's super poisonous. You weren't, by chance, a gardener, were you?"

He shook his head and looked puzzled.

"No, I had a black thumb when I was alive. I could even kill a cactus. I've never heard of that plant before."

"It's super deadly. A tiny amount can be deadly. Can you think of anyone who would've wanted you dead? You can tell me whatever is on your mind. I won't judge, I promise."

He looked uncomfortable and glanced around, spotting Bernie, who was sitting in front of me.

"Is that a cat?"

"Yep, that's Bernie."

He was deflecting, and I thought that was odd. If the positions were reversed and I'd just found out someone poisoned me, I'm pretty sure I would've been shouting for justice and making a list of suspects. To each their own, but something wasn't sitting right with me. I watched him interact with Bernie for a few minutes before pressing ahead.

"Sean, is there anything you'd like to tell me?"

He met my eyes and bunched his shoulders before looking away.

"I don't know. I mean, it's kinda complicated. No, I can't think of anyone who would've wanted me dead, but maybe I didn't know my friends that well."

"Why do you say that?"

"I don't want you to think I'm a bad guy. I mean, you're the only person around here who can talk to me. Unless there are more like you around here?"

I shrugged and shook my head.

"Not that I know of. I promise I won't think less of you. It's more important that we find who killed you and make sure justice is served."

He gave me a wry grin. He wasn't the most handsome guy around, but when he smiled, I could see what the girls saw in him. It was a shame his life had ended so abruptly.

"I was cheating on Trish. There, I said it. Violet and I never really got along, but she came to me when she was having problems with Trevor. It sounds corny, but one thing led to another."

"Did Trish know about it?"

He shook his head.

"No. There's no way she did. I was super careful. It only happened a few times, and we called it off before we came up here."

"Wasn't that awkward?"

"A little. But Violet swore she was going to work on her relationship with Trevor. We agreed that we'd screwed up and swore that it would never happen again."

"So, it was mutual?"

He nodded his head.

"Yeah, we were both fine with it."

"Do you think Trevor knew?"

"I don't think so. Like I said, it only happened a few times. He was out of town for his work when we got together."

"Do you think Trish knew or suspected anything?"

He blew out a breath between pursed lips and I smiled, thinking of how our human mannerisms stay with us, even when we're no longer corporal.

"I don't think so. We'd drifted apart a little, but I was determined to focus on our relationship and put in the work. It sounds weird, but my brief fling with Violet was the best thing that could have happened for Trish and me."

I couldn't help but wonder if Trish would feel that way if she knew.

"Did you plan on asking her to marry you?"

He jerked his head back and gave me a strange look.

"No way. We were not anywhere close to that stage. I mean, we'd been together for a while, but no. I had no plans to ask her that."

I racked my brain, trying to come up with someone else in the group that had a motive to see him dead.

"How about Willow and Seth? Do you think either of them would've killed you?"

He shook his head helplessly, and I noticed he was fading around the edges. Darn it. I still had more questions. Bernie walked a circle around Sean, and I noticed his ghostly form solidified a little.

"No, we were all pretty tight. I've known them forever and we've had no beef."

He faded again, and I looked down at Bernie for help. He met my eyes and blinked at me. I guess he'd done what he could.

"One last question. Please try to hold on. Why were you so worried about Violet when I broke the news to you? What did you want me to tell her?"

His brow furrowed, and he shook his head.

"It's like it's right there, but I can't reach the answer. All I know is when you said that my instinct was to make sure she was okay. I don't know why. I'm sorry. I wanted you to tell her that everything will be okay."

"Anything you'd like me to tell Trish?"

He was nearly transparent, but I could just make out his features. He gave me a half smile and shrugged.

"Sorry, not really."

And with that stellar example of relationship goals I never hoped to achieve, he disappeared. I sat back as Bernie jumped onto my lap and curled up. I stroked his head and thought about what I'd learned.

"It just goes to show that you think you know someone, but you really don't. Trish was so broken up by Sean's death, but he obviously didn't share that same deep emotion, did he?"

Bernie meowed and closed his eyes, lulled by my stroking. I moved my fingers down to his chin, which he jutted out. I could just make out the corners of his lips, turning up in a smile. I looked around the trees and wondered if I'd get lucky enough to see Ned, too.

At least it was a beautiful day and there were worse places to spend a few hours sitting in the sun. I pulled my notebook out of my bag and moved over to the table on the deck, displacing Bernie. He gave me a cranky look before hopping on the table and sitting next to the paper.

"Sorry, bud. I want to write what Sean said so I don't forget."

I was lost in thought, making notes, when I heard a familiar, raspy voice that made me jump. Bernie jerked upright, fur fluffed up to twice his size, and let out a little surprised yowl.

"Whatcha doing there, girly?"

"My goodness, Ned. You can't just sneak up on people like that."

He was sitting in the chair next to me, grinning like a loon. In the bright sunlight, I could make out more of his features. His left shoulder was hunched dramatically, but his beady eyes were bright and kept bouncing between Bernie and me.

"And who says I can't? One of the best things about being a ghost is scaring people."

"It's not polite."

Bernie marched over in front of Ned and sat down, gazing at him. I watched as Ned reacted with a hacking laugh. Could he hear Bernie?

"Now listen here, beastie. I could skin you and wear you as a hat. In fact, your black fur would go nicely with my robe."

Bernie hissed and narrowed his eyes. I watched them both, fascinated by their silent byplay.

"Fine, I'll play nice with your mistress here, but only because I know what you are."

"Wait, what is he? He's a cat. Right?" I asked, breaking into their conversation, unable to keep quiet.

Ned fixed me with his gleaming eyes and spit to the side.

"You don't know? Well, don't that beat all. Not sure if it's my place to say."

"Come on, Ned. What is he?"

Bernie glared at me before returning his attention to Ned, who was shaking his head.

"All I'll say is he's more than you think he is. Nasty sense of humor this beast has, though, that's for sure."

"You can hear him?"

"Plain as day. You can't?"

"No."

I was completely frustrated with this conversation.

"Hmph. That's interesting. Well, I ain't here to help you talk to a cat, I know that."

I took a deep breath, trying to keep my temper under wraps. This was absolutely infuriating.

"Why are you here, Ned?"

"Told you yesterday I saw something. Noticed you were talking with that young kid and figured I'd come eavesdrop. Something doesn't add up."

"What did you see?"

I leaned forward in my chair, desperate for a lead. I wasn't sure if I could trust this ghost, but so far, he could be the only eyewitness to the crime.

"Saw that kid talking with a girl. She gave him something to drink, and they talked a long time. She went inside and then he kinda just fell over, sudden like. The strangest thing."

"What did she look like?"

"Long hair. Shorter than him," Ned said with a shrug. "I paid little attention till he tipped over."

Unfortunately, all three girls matched that description.

"Did you see what happened after that? Who mauled him?"

Ned shook his head and lifted his right shoulder briefly.

"Nope. When I last saw him, he was lying on the grass. I drifted around after that."

"Why were you there? In fact, why have you been appearing here?"

He let out another hacking laugh that turned into a phlegmy cough. I winced, wishing I could pass him the ghostly equivalent of a tissue. He spat to the side, and I closed my eyes out of reflex.

"I dunno. It was the strangest thing. I remember floating around in the other place, having a grand old time, when suddenly I got pulled back here. What year is it, anyway? I'm not used to seeing ladies wearing those things on their legs," he said, gesturing towards my jeans.

"It's 2021," I said. "I think you passed in the late 1800s, if the reports are correct."

He let out a low whistle.

"Is that right? I was away longer than I thought. You know those things show off your backside, right? Not that I'm complaining. In my day, it was all a guessing game. Now, it's all right in front of you."

I shook my head, not wanting to deal with a pervy ghost on a beautiful day like today. Bernie meowed crossly and Ned laughed again.

"Sorry about that. Just stating a fact."

I flapped my hand at him, wanting to get back on track.

"Why do you think you were brought back here? Where were you before?"

"I'm not sure," he said, looking thoughtful. "I miss the other place, though. Learned a lot."

"Like how to move things and make physical sounds?"

He waggled his overgrown eyebrows at me and grinned, exposing a set of discolored, chipped teeth.

"Wouldn't you like to know?"

"Yes, that's why I asked," I said, dryly.

He slapped his knee and leaned back in his chair, a maneuver that was complicated by his misshapen back. I glanced at his shoulder before quickly looking away. It wasn't my place to pry.

"Mining accident. Fell down a shaft and bunged up my back. Been like this ever since," he said, seeming to understand what I didn't want to ask.

"I see. Did you know Herbert Mason?"

His face darkened and suddenly an icy wind picked up, howling around the corner of the building. I looked around and made eye contact with Bernie. His back was hunched, and he was growling quietly. Ned looked abashed, and the wind cut off.

"Sorry about that. My temper got the best of me. Yeah, I knew that no-good, louse-ridden, yellow-bellied, lying sack of...

"So, you weren't a fan, I take it?" I asked, cutting off his string of creative insults.

"You could say that."

"When you came back here from wherever you were before, what made you scare people at this cabin?"

"I reckon it's as good a pastime as any. I wanted to apply what I'd learned. I never realized ghosts could have this much fun. This was all mine, you know? Now there's this fancy cabin sitting here and people are trekking all over the place, acting like they own it. every day, it's different people. It wears on a body. I want them gone."

That reminded me of the presence I'd felt in the attic that told me to get out. I made eye contact with Ned and glared at him.

"Was that you in the attic?"

"Mebbe. Mebbe not," he said, cackling. "Funny how people react, though."

"These people are renting the cabin. It's a thing these days. They come up here, looking for peace and relaxation, not being scared out of their wits by a ghost."

"Don't really care. I get bored. I miss where I was before."

"Do you want to go back? Maybe I could help," I said, watching his face for his reaction.

His beady eyes fastened on me and he licked his lips.

"I reckon you and this beastie of yours probably could. We'll see. I wanna see how this plays out."

He straightened up as much as he could and hauled himself to his feet before disappearing in a gust of wind that knocked the chair over. I startled at the loud sound and looked over at Bernie.

"What did you make of that?"

He chirped quietly before jumping down and loading himself into his bag. I guess our work here was done. I zipped it shut and put the strap over my shoulder, remembering to grab my notebook before we left.

"I've got some questions for you, by the way. How can Ned understand you and I can't? What did he mean when he asked if I knew what you were?"

Bernie's non-committal meow did nothing to ease my curiosity. I sighed and walked back to my car, trying to figure out what my next steps should be.

15

As I turned onto the main road leading down the mountain, I opened the windows to enjoy the crisp mountain air. It was turning out to be a gorgeous day, and I almost wished I could spend more time up here where it would be cooler. I slowed my car as I spotted someone jogging towards me. Now that was dedication. Typically, the only time I was found running was if someone was chasing me, and I certainly wasn't up to running uphill the entire way. No, thank you.

As I got closer, I recognized the woman running and pulled to a stop. I rolled my window down the rest of the way and smiled at the girl.

"Hi, Willow. Beautiful day, isn't it?"

Her pretty face was flushed with exertion, but it didn't look like she'd even broken a sweat. I was a little jealous. Okay, I was a lot jealous. She took out her earbuds as she walked over to my window.

"Hi. Brynn, right?"

"That's me. Getting a little exercise in?"

"Yeah, I'm used to running ten miles a day at home and I had to get out of that cabin. My friends are great, but with all of us cooped up, I couldn't take it anymore."

"Has the Sheriff been up to talk to you?"

She nodded and looked up the hill towards where they were staying.

"Yeah, he was there this morning. He said Sean was poisoned. Do you think he came across something in the woods?"

She looked around at the nearby foliage as if it was waiting to ambush her at any moment.

"I'm not sure," I said, not wanting to tip her off that the poison was rare.

"It's just so weird. If he was poisoned, why did he end up all mauled? I never got a good look at him after... after he was found, but from Trish's reaction, it was pretty bad. Unless you think an animal got to him after the fact? The Sheriff said we were safe and could leave the cabin as long as we didn't leave town, but I never thought about that. "

Her face was open, and she didn't appear to be hiding anything. She looked as perplexed as I felt. Unless she was a world-class actress, my gut told me she was innocent.

"Do you think one of your friends could've killed him?"

She looked surprised and her brow wrinkled up a bit as she shook her head.

"I don't know. I wouldn't think so. We were all pretty close. It's just crazy. Here we are, all coming up in the world together with big plans for the future. And now? Sean's gone. I just don't understand it."

I couldn't help but notice she really hadn't answered my question. Did she know more than she was putting on? Bernie hopped onto my lap and stuck his head out the window. Willow's face brightened, and she reached a hand up before pausing.

"Is it okay if I pet him?"

"Go ahead."

Bernie nudged her hand with his head and she had a sweet smile on her face as she gently stroked between his ears.

"Cool cat. I didn't know you could take cats in cars. I thought they always hated it."

"Bernie's pretty chill. Do you know if any of the girls in your group are into anything like witchcraft?"

She seemed taken aback by my left-field question and her hand paused on Bernie's head before resuming.

"I don't think so. I mean, I'd assume I'd know something like that. We see each other all the time. Violet's always been a little new-agey, I guess. If any of them were closet witches, I guess she could be."

She shrugged and gave Bernie another pat before stepping back from the window.

"Is there anything else you remember about the night Sean was killed?"

She looked off towards the cabin again and bit her lip.

"There is something, but I'm not sure."

"Anything, even if it seems small, might matter."

"Well, I remember waking up in the middle of the night. Our bedroom is right next to the bathroom, and I swear I heard the shower turn on. It woke me, but I went right back to sleep. I don't know, maybe I was just dreaming."

"How long would you say it was between hearing that and hearing Trish screaming?"

She reset her pony tail holder as she thought, still biting on her lip.

"I honestly couldn't say. I'm sorry. I was really out of it that night," she said as she finished tying up her hair. "I could be totally mistaken, too."

"Did you tell the Sheriff about that?"

"No, I didn't think of that until just now. Do you think I should call him?"

"I can pass it along. I'll let you get back to your run. If you think of anything else, please call me. Day or night, it doesn't matter."

She nodded as she put her earbuds back in.

"Will do. I need to get back. We're all planning on heading into town for a few hours. It's been awful being cramped up in that cabin."

"Willow, be careful. Okay?"

She gave me a sunny smile and a wave as she headed up the road.

I started my car again as Bernie leapt over the console and got settled in the passenger seat.

"What do you think, Bern? Do you think she was telling the truth?"

He blinked at me before turning to look out the window.

"Well, let's go see if we can find out if Zane learned anything about their backgrounds. I'm not sure what else to do at this point."

I drove down the mountain and headed towards home, lost in thought. Willow said Violet was into new-age stuff, but that didn't mean she was the one who killed Sean. Did it? I shook my head. I needed more information. My phone rang as I pulled onto my street and I smiled when I saw the screen.

"Zane, just the person I wanted to talk to."

His warm chuckle made me smile as I turned into my driveway.

"Are you home? I found out a few interesting things and I'm about ten minutes from your house."

"Just pulled in. Want to have an early lunch?"

"Perfect. I'll grab a few sandwiches from the deli. What's your favorite?"

I thought for a second, debating the benefits of roast beef over pastrami before settling for the beef. I gave him my order and signed off before grabbing Bernie's carrier and heading inside. I spotted the abstract sitting on the table and sat down to read through it again until Zane showed up.

Bernie joined me at the table and looked over my shoulder as I read. He pawed at my laptop and I remembered I wanted to see if there was any link between Herbert and Trent Mason.

"Good idea, buddy. Let's see what we can find."

I pulled up a genealogy site and typed in Herbert Mason. A little cheer escaped as I saw there were a few family trees available. I clicked on the first one and read through it, not seeing Trent's name. I backed out of the page and went to the next one. This one was much more detailed and as I scrolled down the page, I spotted Trent's name.

"Yes! He is related, Bernie. It looks like he's a cousin of some sorts."

I was never good at figuring out degrees of separation and got tangled up somewhere with third and fourth cousins, but Trent's name was definitely there. I closed the laptop and added to my case notes.

Now that I knew there was an actual connection, Ned's re-appearance made more sense. He said he'd been pulled into this reality a few months ago and it coincided with Trent's purchase of the property. Was it possible his spirit had somehow sensed the return of his old rival's relative? It seemed preposterous, but one thing I'd learned is that with the spirit world, nearly anything is possible. A knock on the door startled me and I jumped up and opened the door.

"There's my girl," Zane said, kissing me on the cheek as he walked past. "Sorry I got delayed at the deli, there was a big line."

"No worries. I got lost going through Herbert Mason's family tree," I said as I followed him to the kitchen and grabbed some plates.

"What did you find out?"

"The new owner is definitely related, but it's pretty distant. Still, the timeline matches up. I don't really understand it, but it's interesting."

We plated up our sandwiches and headed back to the table to enjoy our lunch. While we ate, I told Zane about Sean's ghost and what I'd learned from Ned. He perked up when I mentioned Willow hearing the shower turn on.

"I'm guessing whoever killed Sean had to get cleaned up before they could 'discover' the body," he said, using air quotes. "Who found him?"

"Trish. She woke everyone up with her screams. She seems so upset by his death, though. I don't think she could fake that. She was genuinely distraught. I don't think she's the one who killed him."

Zane shook his head as he finished up his sandwich.

"Maybe whoever did it just waited until someone else could find him. That could've happened."

"What did you learn about their backgrounds?" I asked, keeping a small piece of roast beef for Bernie.

"Not much. They're all pretty clean. The only thing that came up was Violet was sent to juvenile detention, but those records are sealed."

"Sealed, huh? Hmmm. I wonder what could have happened there?"

"I wish we could find out. A few of them had a couple parking tickets and a speeding violation, here or there, but nothing that would show someone with a violent past."

Bernie bumped my leg, and I passed down the roast beef to him. He snapped it up and then stared at me. I thought about what Ned said, that he was more than just a cat, but decided not to pass that information on to Zane. He was dealing with enough. I still didn't know what to make of it. Bernie kept staring at me and I shook my head, frustrated that I couldn't understand him. I took the plates and walked into the kitchen. Bernie followed close by me and leaned against my leg while I rinsed off the dishes. I reached down to pet him and had a thought.

"Zane, Willow said they were all planning on coming into town for a few hours today."

Zane quirked an eyebrow.

"And...?"

"Well, since you're now a consultant with the Sheriff's office, we could go up to the cabin while it's empty and do some looking around? I can get the code from Liz, I'm sure of it."

"I don't know, Brynn. That plan feels like a lot of things could go wrong."

I walked over to the table and sat across from him.

"It will be fine! We'll be in and out. One of them has to be hiding something. This is the best way to find out."

"Do you think Dave would appreciate us doing this? We could muck up the chain of evidence."

"I think he'll be fine with it. We won't touch anything, we'll just look. If we find something, we can let him know. Then he can get a warrant."

"I'm not sure this is a good idea."

"It will be fine. Tell you what, I'll even call him first. Will that help?"

Zane's shoulders slumped, and he gave me a look that said I was close to wearing him down.

"If you tell Dave, I'll feel better about it."

"Score!"

I dialed Dave's number and waited not so patiently for him to pick up. I got up and started pacing back and forth as the phone rang. It finally went to voicemail, and I left a hurried message. I ended the call and texted Liz, asking if she could give me the code for the cabin where everyone was staying, and crossed my fingers. I knew this was the break we were looking for.

Zane shook his head and walked up behind me, wrapping his muscular arms around my waist. I'd like to think it was because he was feeling romantic, but honestly, I was probably irritating him. Bernie sat by his carrier, waiting expectantly.

"Brynn, if you want to do this, we'll do it. I just want to keep you safe."

"We'll be fine. Yes, Liz just answered," I said, holding up my phone so he could see. "She obviously doesn't have a problem with it."

He rolled his eyes and followed me to the door, pausing when his phone rang. I zipped up Bernie's bag after he darted into it and resisted pacing again as we waited for Zane.

His face looked thunderous as he talked to whoever was on the other line. He tucked his hair behind his ear and ended the call.

"Pump the brakes. That was my client. They've got an issue and I need to go down there right away."

"The place where you put in the cameras? I thought you talked to them about it yesterday."

"I did, but this guy is needy. Brynn, I've got to go. I know you won't like this, but..."

"But they're only going to be in town for a few hours. We may not get this opportunity again."

He pinched the skin between his eyebrows and let out an enormous sigh.

"I won't talk you out of this, will I?"

"Nope."

"Will you at least see if Logan can go with you? I don't want you going back up there alone."

"I'm not alone, I've got Bernie."

"No offense, but what's Bernie going to do?"

From the enraged meow coming from the carrier, it sure sounded like Zane found his way onto Bernie's list.

"Fine. I'll see if Logan can come with me. If he can't, we'll regroup. I'll be smart."

Zane kissed me on the forehead and pulled me in for a hard hug.

"Please. My heart can't take it if something else happens to you. I know this is important to you, but your safety is important to me."

I melted a little as he spoke. Okay, I turned into a big puddle of goo. This guy was something else.

"I'll be careful. Call me as soon as you're done with Mr. Needy."

He groaned as he headed out the door.

"This is one job I probably shouldn't have taken."

I watched him walk down the sidewalk before dialing Logan's number. I crossed my fingers as I waited for him to pick up.

"Freckles! What's up?"

I did a little dance when I heard his voice and quickly described what I needed from him. The line went quiet.

"Logan? Are you still there?"

"I'm here, but I don't know what to say. You want me to go break and enter a cabin with you?"

"It's not really breaking and entering. I told Dave what we're doing, and Liz gave me the code, so... I'd call it a fact finding mission. Please say you will. Zane doesn't want me going up there alone."

"Well, if it will make him happy, I'm all for that. Does this mean a lot to you, Copper Top?"

"It does."

He heaved a sigh.

"I'll be there in ten minutes. Let me get my guys lined out. We can go up there in my truck."

"Thank you. Logan. I owe you. Big time."

He let out an evil laugh, and I rolled my eyes, knowing I was in for it when he collected. I ended the call and let Bernie out of his bag while we waited. I had a feeling we were about to uncover something big.

16

I was practically vibrating with impatience by the time I saw Logan's pickup pull to a stop in front of my house. Bernie seemed to sense my mood and loaded himself into his bag before I could even ask. I had him zipped up and was out the door by the time Logan opened his door. He quirked an eyebrow at me as I slid into the passenger side breathlessly.

"Where's the fire?"

I flapped a hand at him.

"There's no fire, but I don't know how much time we have until everyone gets back to the cabin. Let's go!"

He shook his head as he fired the truck back up and drove towards the highway.

"Okay, why is this so important, again?"

I launched into my tale, summing up what I'd learned since the last time we talked. The last thing I wanted to do was get stuck in the cabin when Sean's friends returned. One of them was likely the murderer, and I did not want to end up dead. There had been too many close calls lately. In and out, that was my goal. Logan listened and nodded before shooting me a grin.

"So, we're basically breaking into this place and snooping around?"

"No, we're entering with a code given to us by the property manager. Big difference."

"If you say so. How are things with Zane?"

I couldn't help smiling as I looked out the window. I'd never imagined meeting someone like Zane and from the butterflies in my stomach, I was pretty sure I was falling in love with the guy. Okay, okay, I was head over heels, but I wasn't quite ready to admit that yet. Especially to my cousin, who was sure to spread the news to his mom, which would end up getting to my mom in record time. I wasn't ready to cross that bridge just yet.

"It's good. Fantastic. How's Kelsie?"

The tips of Logan's ears turned red, and I bit my lip, determined not to tease him too much. He'd played the field for so long, I'd been convinced he wouldn't find someone special. Who would have thought the girl who used to tease me in high school might just be the one for him? Luckily, we'd all matured, and she'd turned into a much nicer person than I ever thought she could be.

"It's good. We're taking things slow."

I narrowed my eyes at him.

"And that's okay, right? You're cool with that?"

He gave me a sheepish smile and ducked his head a little.

"Yeah, it's all good."

"I'm proud of you, Logan."

"Oh geez, let's not get all mushy. Kelsie's a nice girl. I'm looking forward to getting to know her better. We've all changed a bunch since we were in school. You're sure you're still okay with it?"

"Of course. I actually like her. I never thought I'd say that, but there it is. I think she'll be good for you."

He rolled his eyes and focused on the winding mountain road.

"Well, as long as you think that. Where's the cabin?"

I gave him the directions and looked down at Bernie in his bag. Logan's truck was full of tools and I didn't want to risk Bernie getting injured accidentally, so I'd left him zipped in. He wasn't thrilled, but hey, sometimes being a cat mom means making tough decisions. He made eye contact with me and narrowed his green eyes, glaring for all he was worth.

"Bernie, I'm just being safe."

If I could read his mind, I'm pretty sure he said 'whatever' before sniffing and turning away from me. Cats.

We pulled to a stop in front of the cabin and I looked around. No cars. This was a good sign. I grabbed Bernie's bag and jumped down.

"Okay, we have little time. Let's divide up and search the three rooms. If you find anything suspicious, let me know."

Logan trotted after me.

"Define suspicious."

"Anything that could maul someone so badly, it looked like a wild animal got them. And poison. Any plant material or powder that doesn't look normal."

His eyebrows flew up, and he stopped in his tracks.

"Um, Brynn. I don't know about this."

"It will be fine. In and out."

I punched in the code and walked in, calling out to make sure we were alone. After a few seconds of silence, I let Bernie out of his carrier and he shot out like he'd been fired from a cannon.

"Try not shed, Bernie."

He didn't even bother to glance back at me. Figures. Well, hopefully they wouldn't notice the black cat hair he would inevitably leave behind. I turned to Logan and smiled, noticing he looked uncomfortable. He ran a hand through his hair and shook his head.

"The things I do for you, cousin."

"I owe you one. You take that room over there, and I'll take this one. We can check the last one together."

I walked into the room where I'd seen Trish and looked around. A suitcase sat in the middle of the floor and nothing felt out of place. The room was clean, like super clean. I opened the drawers on the dresser but found nothing. She was the type who lived out of a suitcase instead of unpacking. Good to know. I checked under the bed and nearly fell over backward when Bernie shot out from underneath there. I glimpsed his tail as he ran out of the room.

"Geez, cat. You nearly gave me a heart attack."

I went back to my search and paused when I got to her bag. Did I really want to go through her personal things? The poor girl had lost her boyfriend and here I was rummaging through her stuff. Still, I needed to rule her out. I went through her clothes quickly, making sure I left everything as I found it. Nothing.

I walked into the attached bathroom and looked around. It was even tidier than the bedroom. No hair products or clutter on the counter. It looked sterile. I backed out of the small room and headed into the hallway, where I bumped into Logan.

"Anything? Which room did you take?"

"The far one down there. A couple is in there, but that's all I could tell you. It was a mess. Looked like a tornado went through there five minutes before I walked in. From what I could tell, there wasn't anything suspicious."

"Okay, that leaves this room," I said, pointing at the one in the middle. "Let's hurry."

I led the way into the room. I wasn't sure which couple was in here, but they were relatively tidy. I ducked into the bathroom and saw a multitude of bottles on the counter. From the labels, I figured this had to be Violet of the split ends domain. I glanced around, but saw nothing out of the ordinary. As I poked my head back out of the bathroom, I saw Logan gingerly going through the bags on the floor.

"Nothing, Brynn. No knives, no creepy poison. Just normal stuff."

"Okay, let's try the kitchen."

I walked out of the room and looked around for Bernie before heading into the kitchen. Logan joined me and we went through the cabinets and drawers, one by one. Nothing looked out of place and I straightened up, frustrated. I was just about to say something to Logan when I heard a vehicle in the drive. Logan and I froze. This was not good. I needed to come up with a plausible excuse for our presence, and fast. The door swung open and Trish walked in, stopping short when she saw us.

"What are you doing here?" she asked, hand snaking into her purse.

I elbowed Logan in the side and held up my hands, hoping he'd turn on his invincible charm while I tried to talk us out of this situation.

"Trish, it's good to see you. I came up to see if you guys would mind if I asked a few more questions. The door was open, and we thought someone was here. I was just about to leave a note. Oh, this is Logan, my cousin. He's my ride today."

Hopefully, she wouldn't notice Bernie's bag sitting behind her. Trish's hand relaxed and fell to her side as she walked to the kitchen.

"I see. Sorry, everyone else is in town. I was tired of shopping and came back early."

She nodded at Logan and walked to the fridge.

"Do you think the others will be back soon?"

She shrugged as she grabbed a pitcher of iced tea and put it on the counter.

"I don't know. Do you guys want some tea?"

I glanced over at Logan before nodding.

"Sure, that would be great. How are you doing?"

She poured out three glasses and slid two in our direction.

"I'm taking it day by day. It's just so hard. I keep waking up thinking it was all just a bad dream. But it's not. This is my new reality."

Logan sipped from his tea and cleared his throat before asking her a question.

"Were you with Sean for a long time?"

"Yeah. We were about to get engaged."

I thought back to what Sean said about there not being any chance of them getting married as I took a drink of the tea. It tasted too sweet, and I grimaced before setting the glass back down on the counter. Logan took another drink and leaned against the counter.

"I'm sorry to hear that. Do you know when the funeral service will be?"

She crossed her arms over her chest and shook her head, long hair flying.

"I don't know. They won't tell us when they're going to release the body. I've talked to his mom. She's in Florida, but she's trying to get a flight out here for tomorrow. I couldn't reach her for a couple days."

I cocked my head as Logan took another drink of his tea, finishing it. It seemed odd that his mom hadn't been notified by the police.

"Didn't Dave notify his next of kin?"

She shook her head again and wiped at her eyes.

"I told him I'd do it. Sean's mom is pretty delicate, and I wanted the bad news to come from someone close to the family."

My lips felt numb, and I bit into the top one, trying to focus on my next question.

"Did Dave tell you the cause of Sean's death?"

"You should have some more tea. It's great. I made it myself."

My heart felt like it was going to beat out of my chest and I grabbed the counter, shaking my head to clear it. I realized she hadn't answered my question.

"No thanks, I'm not a fan of sweet tea," I said, glancing over at Logan.

His face was flushed and beads of sweat were visible on his forehead. I stepped towards him as he slumped further on the counter.

"Logan!"

I heard a drawer open and turned just in time to see Trish standing there with a rolling pin before everything went black.

* * *

WHEN I OPENED MY EYES, the room wobbled a little around the edges before coming into focus. Bernie was lying on my chest, licking my face furiously. He chirped and stepped off my chest, hurrying to my left. I wasn't sure how he'd gotten back in here without Trish knowing, but I'd never been happier to see him. I glanced around my surroundings and found Logan lying flat on the floor next to me.

"Oh my God. Logan!"

I shook him, but he didn't wake up. I felt for his pulse and relaxed a little when I could feel his heartbeat. It was fast and faint, but it was there. A sharp pain shot through my head as I pulled myself up. Bernie sat on Logan's chest and started licking his face as I held my head in my hands and tried to get my wayward brain to work.

"Bernie, what do we do?"

He shot me a look, and I wished like I never had before that we could communicate. He closed his eyes and went back to licking Logan.

I looked around the room, confirming it was Trish's, and groaned as all the pieces fell together. There was a reason her suitcase was neatly packed, and she'd left her friends early. Sure enough, the suitcase was gone. The only question was if she was coming back to finish the job? Why had we been so stupid and taken the iced tea?

I felt for my phone in my pocket and cursed softly when I realized it was gone. I checked Logan's pocket and cursed again. I felt for his pulse as my mind raced. How were we going to get out of this?

I'd called Dave and let him know what we were doing, but would he check his messages? Would he think it was necessary to come up here? Zane might check on us, but that could be hours away. I needed to get us out of here and get Logan to the hospital. He'd had a full glass of the tea, while I'd just had a sip.

I made my way to the door, trying to get my limbs to work properly. It was locked and there wasn't a way to unlock it from this side. A faint thought about how that probably wasn't code flitted through my head as I looked around for another way out. The window in the room was all that was left. Even though we were on the second story, I needed to haul my cousin out of here and get us to safety.

I staggered over to the window and pulled it up as wide as it would go. It was small, but I thought it would be just wide enough to pull Logan through. I glanced down and gulped, not liking how far the drop was. I grabbed the screen and worked it back and forth until it finally popped free. An icy wind blew through the room, and the hair on the back of my neck stood up. A familiar voice sounded from behind me.

"Looks like you're in a spot of trouble, girly."

17

The crusty miner's eyes gleamed out from his bearskin rug and I swallowed a whoop of joy. Ned was just the person, er ghost, I needed to see.

"How did you know I was here?" I asked.

He nodded his head towards Bernie, who was still trying to revive Logan.

"That one there called to me. I haven't been in these parts since, oh, probably right before I died. Sure has changed a lot. I should expand my horizons more. Plenty of people over on this side of the mountain to scare."

He looked around and rubbed his hands together, cackling with glee. I bit my tongue to keep my temper under wraps. Now was not the time to irritate this spirit. With my luck, he'd disappear.

"Right. So, I need help," I said, trying gently to get him back on track.

"Who's this fella?"

"That's Logan, my cousin. He's been poisoned, and we need to get him to a doctor. Our phones are gone and we're locked in here. I was getting ready to drag him out through the window when you showed up."

He eyed my scrawny arms doubtfully, and I tossed my hands in the air, completely frustrated.

"Now, don't go getting all weepy on me, girly. Who locked you in here?"

"The girl you saw the night Sean died. She's the one who killed him."

"And you let her poison you? I thought you were smarter than that."

Bernie let out a cross-sounding yowl and trotted over, staring at Ned. They stared at one another and I tried to keep from shifting in impatience. We needed to get out of here. Ned cocked his head to the side and then looked down at Bernie.

"And you think that will work? Alright, beastie. If you say so."

"Say what? What's he saying?" I asked.

Ned floated towards me and pointed his finger at my head. I looked at him, thoroughly confused by what was going on. He looked over at Bernie again. My cat gave a solemn nod and Ned came closer, his finger right in front of my forehead. He squeezed his eyes shut and poked me hard, right between the eyes.

"Ow! What was that for?" I asked, rubbing my forehead and looking between the two.

"Brynn, get a hold of yourself. I swear you are terrible in these situations and yet you insist on getting into them constantly. Honestly, it's almost too much to take," Bernie said, glowering at me.

"Wait. How? Who?"

Bernie rolled his eyes as Ned cackled again, spinning around the room with delight.

"That's not important. What's important is getting Logan to a doctor. I've done what I can and I've stabilized him, but he needs professional help."

"Apparently, he's not the only one," I said, half under my breath. "I must still be dreaming."

If a cat could snap its toes, Bernie would have. He stomped over and stood in front of me, lashing his tail.

"Get it together, woman. Ned, check to see if that crazy witch is still in the house. I don't hear her, but it's smart to check. Brynn, keep trying to wake Logan up. I'll see what I can do about the door."

"Yessir," I said, dazed and totally confused as I obeyed my cat's orders.

Ned floated through the wall and I looked down at Logan's pale face. He'd stopped sweating, but I didn't know if that was a good thing. I gently tapped on his cheek, hoping he'd wake up.

"Logan. Can you hear me?"

"Really? You're just going to tap on his cheek? Come on, Brynn. We have little time. He's too big for you to carry out of here. If you don't wake him up, I will," Bernie said, flashing the claws on his right paw before returning his focus to the door.

I wasn't sure what he was doing, and I didn't want to ask. I'd always known Bernie was special, but I didn't know just how much he could do. I returned my focus to Logan and slapped him hard across the cheek, wincing at the loud noise my palm made as it hit his cheek.

"Brynn?"

Logan's eyes fluttered open. Relief flooded through my body and tears started pouring down my cheeks.

"Oh my God, you're awake. I thought you were going to die."

He tried to lift his hand to his cheek, but he must have been too weak. He settled for a soft chuckle.

"Geez, you didn't need to hit me that hard if you thought I was dying. What happened?"

Ned floated back through the wall and Logan startled. I looked between them.

"Can you see Ned?"

"Um, if that guy over there wearing a bear is Ned, then yes, I guess I can see him."

He shook his head as if to clear it and closed his eyes again. I hoped his sudden ability to see ghosts didn't mean he was close to joining Ned on the other side.

"Did you see her, Ned?" I asked.

"Sure didn't girly. No one's around."

A loud click came from the door and Bernie's shoulders slumped slightly. I ran over to him and scooped him up in my arms.

"You did it! Are you okay, Bernie?"

He gave my cheek a lick with his raspy tongue before settling his head on my shoulder. His small body felt limp in my arms and my heart clenched.

"Logan, let's go. Ned, thank you. I'll be back up at the cabin once it's safe. I've got to get these guys to town."

Ned tipped his hat at me as whirled around the room, before popping out of sight. I went back to Logan and held a hand out to help him get to his feet. His face was still pale, and he swayed alarmingly before almost falling down. I raced around his side and put one of his arms over my shoulder.

"Sorry, Brynn. I don't know why I feel so weak. What was in that tea?"

"I'm afraid it was oleander, but since you're still alive, maybe not. Why did you drink the whole glass?" I asked as we bumped our way to the front door.

"I was thirsty."

I looked around the kitchen, hoping she'd left our phones, but I couldn't see them. I couldn't afford to waste any more time. I stopped to grab Bernie's bag with and we made our way slowly back to Logan's truck. I helped him inside before passing Bernie to him. He cradled him to his chest, and I noticed the sweat was beading on his forehead again. I ran around the front of the truck and hopped in, throwing it in reverse and tearing down the driveway.

The hospital was about twenty minutes away, and from the look on Logan's face, I wasn't sure I had that long. I sped through the resort area and headed down the hill, going as fast as I could without flying off the road. I checked my rearview mirror and looked over at Logan and Bernie.

Bernie's head came up, and I saw those beautiful green eyes looking at me and nearly cried.

"You're doing great, Brynn. Just keep believing in yourself."

"Hey, where's the snark?" I asked, wiping away a tear that slipped past my defenses.

He gave a soft chirp and whispered.

"Maybe later. I need a nap. That lock took everything out of me."

I fishtailed the truck around a corner and Logan's head hit the passenger window with a shallow thud.

"Sorry!"

He didn't respond. I gritted my teeth and added more speed, determined to get off this stupid mountain and back to civilization. A car zoomed past me, going the other way, and I glanced in my rearview mirror as it slid to a stop before whipping behind me. You've got to be kidding me.

I sped up, and the car matched my acceleration. I glanced back in my mirror and swallowed hard when I recognized the driver. Trish was back and, from the looks of it, she was not happy to see we'd escaped.

I went around the last corner and skidded onto the highway, almost losing control. Trish's car made the curve without a problem.

"Geez, is this girl a Nascar car driver or something?"

I mashed the pedal to the floor and the truck shot forward, engine roaring. The distance between our vehicles grew, and I kept it up, trusting that Logan's big truck could eventually outrun her car. As we went around another curve, I spotted flashing blue and red lights, and glimpsed Dave's face as we flew past his truck.

I said a quiet prayer that he'd recognize the situation and kept speeding down the road. His truck nipped in right behind Trish and I could almost feel her indecision as our eyes met in my mirror. She made an ugly face and spun her wheel, spinning into the other lane. I slowed as I watched Dave's truck slam to a stop and follow her. I'd never wished for my phone more in that moment, but I knew Dave would radio for help. I stayed in my lane and kept going, willing the truck to go faster.

Within a few minutes, the welcome sight of the hospital ahead took my breath away. I looked over at Logan.

"We're here. Hang on for me."

He didn't answer. I crammed on the brakes and came to a shuddering stop at the entrance to the emergency room before hopping out of the truck and racing around to the passenger side. A man wearing scrubs banged through the doors, swearing loudly.

"What are you thinking coming in hot like that?" he asked, face red.

"I'm sorry, but my cousin needs help. He's been poisoned."

The man shouted over his shoulder and immediately helped me get Logan out of the seat. More people streamed out through the doors, rolling a gurney. I grabbed Bernie and watched as they lifted Logan onto it and pushed him inside at a full run. I trailed behind, trying to keep up as one man shouted a question at me.

"What was he poisoned with?"

"I think it was oleander, but I'm not sure. Is he going to make it?"

The man's face was grim as he trotted alongside the gurney.

"We'll do our best."

Orders were shouted back and forth, and they disappeared into a room with Logan. I stood there, cradling my cat and feeling lost. A woman to my right called out to me, startling me out of my thoughts.

"Miss, are you with the patient they just brought in?"

"Yes, he's my cousin."

"I'm going to need some information. We don't normally allow cats in here, though."

I looked down at my sleeping cat and tightened my arms.

"He won't bother anyone."

She looked doubtful, but shrugged and beckoned for me to come closer. A stack of forms on a clipboard appeared as if by magic, and she slid it across the desk to me.

"I'll need these filled out with as much information as you can provide. Take a seat over there."

She nodded towards the small waiting room. I went to walk that way before remembering Zane. I turned back to her and tried to put on a smile I didn't feel.

"Can I use your phone? Please?"

"Sure, what number do you want me to dial?"

I rattled off Zane's number and waited breathlessly as she handed me the receiver.

"Matthews Security Service, this is Zane."

"Zane, it's Brynn. I'm at the hospital in Deadwood."

He swore loudly, and I pulled the phone away from my ear for a second.

"Are you okay? Please tell me you're okay."

"I'm fine. It's Logan."

"I'll be there in ten minutes."

He ended the call, and I limply handed the phone back to the curious woman behind the desk. I shook my head as I grabbed the clipboard and headed for the waiting room. I found the closest chair and dropped into it, feeling as if all of my bones had suddenly vacated my body. Bernie stirred in my arms and I gently placed him in my lap, stroking his head.

I forced myself to focus on the forms and tried not to let my mind wander down the path of what ifs. Logan was practically a brother to me and although he sometimes annoyed me to no end, he'd been with me my whole life. I bit back a sob as I thought about how he always teased me he was five months older and therefore far more superior. I wiped away my tears and filled out the last form.

Bernie woke up as I stood and I carefully put him on a chair before walking back to the desk and handing over the forms.

"Have you heard anything?" I asked.

She shook her head and gave me a sympathetic look.

"No, but I'm sure they're doing everything they can. As soon as he's stabilized, they'll let you know."

I went back and joined Bernie, mindlessly staring out the window. I'm not sure how long I sat there, but the next thing I knew, Zane was there, pulling me into his muscular arms and crushing me to his chest.

"Oh my God, you're okay," he said, his voice muffled by my hair as he buried his face in the top of my head.

"I'm fine. But Logan..."

"It will be okay. If I know anything about him, he's a fighter. What happened?"

He released me from a hug and scooped Bernie out of the chair before sitting down. He cradled him gently, and I tried to keep it together long enough to tell him about our run in with Trish. His face darkened when I got to the part about the rolling pin and he touched my hair, looking for a wound.

"I'm okay," I said, trying to squirm out of reach.

"Brynn, you were hit in the head. You need to have that looked at."

"No, they need to focus on Logan. After I know he's okay..." I said, taking a deep breath. "After that, I'll let them check me out."

As I finished up my story, the man I'd talked to walked out from the room they'd taken Logan into. He looked around, and I stood up, waving to get his attention.

"I'm sorry, I didn't catch your name in the chaos," he said.

"I'm Brynn Sullivan. Logan's my cousin. This is my boyfriend, Zane Matthews."

He nodded at Zane before continuing.

"Your cousin should make a full recovery. We've pumped him full of activated charcoal and his heart rate has returned to normal."

"Can I see him?"

He shook his head.

"It will be a few hours before he can see anyone. I'm sorry."

"No, I understand. Thank you for helping him."

"I'll come get you when he's ready."

He nodded again and walked away and I sank back into my chair, feeling lighter than air. Bernie stirred in Zane's arms as he sat next to me. One emerald eye cracked open, and he yawned, exposing all of his tiny dagger teeth.

"At least you had some sense when you picked this one," Bernie said. "He knows how to hold a cat properly."

"You've got that right," I said, reaching over to ruffle his fur.

"What's that?" Zane asked, looking confused.

My hand froze on Bernie's head, and I shared a glance with him.

I'd only been able to talk with him for an hour and I'd already blown our cover. I had no way of knowing if whatever Ned had done to me would last, but I didn't feel right keeping things from Zane. I took a deep breath and plowed ahead, hoping this wouldn't be the straw that broke the camel's proverbial back.

"I may have left something out about what happened earlier."

18

By the time I was done telling Zane about being able to hear Bernie, I was worried about his reaction. Luckily, or unluckily, depending on how you look at it, Dave walked in and interrupted our conversation. I held Bernie close as Dave walked up, tipping his hat, before sitting across from us.

He took his hat off and folded the brim with his hands as he glanced between us.

"Since you're out here, I'm gonna guess Logan's still back there?" he asked, nodding his head towards the doors.

"He is. They said he's gonna be okay, though. He's lucky," I said. "I'm so sorry I was speeding like that. Please tell me you caught Trish."

He sat back in the chair and balanced his cowboy hat on his knee before nodding slowly.

"We captured one Patricia Fowler, and right now we've booked her on evading. I'm guessing you have a few more things that can be added to that list? Why on earth was she chasing after you?"

As I told Dave about our crazy afternoon, Zane stood and left the waiting area. Part of me wondered if he was coming back. He'd eventually accepted my ability to talk to ghosts, and I think he truly believed in what I could do. But talking to my cat? Was that a bridge too far? I shook off the thought and focused back on Dave, making sure I left nothing out. I finished my story and Zane reappeared, carrying three bottles of water.

"I thought everyone could use something to drink, but the coffee from the machine smelled like it had been sitting in there for about five years."

"I've had it before. It's more like ten," Dave said as he twisted off the top of his bottle and took a long swig. "Thanks, son."

Zane put his arm around me and pulled me closer to him.

"I'm hoping you'll be able to press charges for attempted murder for what she tried to do to Brynn and Logan. Let alone murdering her boyfriend."

"I'll need to talk to Logan's doctor and make sure the poison was the same. If it was, I think we've got a decent case against her."

"Do you think she'll confess?" I asked, resting my head on Zane's shoulder.

"She was ranting and raving about you ruining everything when I cuffed her," Dave said before he took another drink. "I think she might if it will mean a lesser sentence. We've got our work cut out for us, though. I'll need to bring in her roommates and question them as well."

"At least we know who did it," I said, yawning widely.

I blushed and scrubbed my face, trying to wake up. Dave shook his head and looked out the window.

"Who would've thought a pretty girl like her would be the one responsible? You saw the body, Brynn. She did a number on on him."

I raised my hand to my head and rubbed where Trish had whacked me.

"You need to have this looked at," Zane said.

"The next time the doctor comes out, I'll say something. Do you really think Logan is going to be okay?"

Zane kissed me on the top of my head.

"I'm sure of it. You Sullivans are tough as nails."

"That's the truth of it, right there," Dave said. "I'll never forget the first time I met you two. You got right in the middle of that murder case and refused to stop. Logan defended you each step of the way. Afterwards, too. I know it wasn't easy. Heck, it took me a long time to come to terms with it and I had clear evidence right in front of me."

"Logan's the best. You don't think he'll have any permanent damage, do you?"

Dave levered himself out of the chair and placed his hat back on his head before draining his water bottle.

"I think he'll be fine. I've got to get back to work. You get that noggin of yours looked at, okay? I know you don't want to hear it, but it's better safe than sorry."

"Do you need me to come down and make an official report?"

"We'll talk about that tomorrow. I've got enough to get the ball rolling. I'll call when I need you to come in. Hopefully she'll confess and we'll figure out why and how she did it."

He gave a salute as he walked through the automatic doors of the Emergency Room. I looked down at Bernie and scratched his head, well aware that there was still an elephant in the room between Zane and I. I leaned back so I could see his face and took a deep breath.

"So, about what I said earlier..."

He held my hand and looked into my eyes. I was almost afraid to look back, fearing I'd see judgment there, but all I saw was appreciation and wonder.

"I think it's awesome. I've always said Bernie was a special cat. Do you think it will last?"

I hadn't considered that whatever Ned did to enable me to talk to Bernie would wear off. I looked down at my sleeping cat and swallowed hard.

"I sure hope it will. We've talked before, you know."

Zane cocked his head to the side. I told him about my previous experiences in the in-between as we waited for Logan's doctor to come back out. The light was fading as the sun dipped behind the mountain that shielded the town of Deadwood to the west. We were sitting quietly, hand in hand, as the doctor came out.

"Miss Sullivan, you can see Logan now."

I jumped up and Zane cleared his throat, standing next to me.

"Doc, would you mind looking Brynn over first? She got hit on the head and I'm worried about her."

The doctor leaned closer to me and looked into my eyes. I smiled, not wanting to make a big deal out of it, and waved my hands.

"It's not a big deal. Just a little rolling pin."

"Come with me. There's an examination room around the corner. You'll need to leave the cat behind though."

Zane took Bernie from my arms and I followed the doctor, glancing back at him over my shoulder. He smiled and shook his head before taking a seat with Bernie.

"Really, I'm fine. I feel great. Just a little tired and shaky."

"Did you have any of the iced tea that your cousin drank?"

"Only a sip. It was way too sweet for me."

"That probably saved both of your lives."

I followed him into the room and sat on the examination table, wishing I could just go see Logan. I sat through a battery of simple tests and the doctor finally nodded after he shined a bright light in my eyes and had me follow his finger.

"I think you're okay. You must have a hard head."

"I've been told that a time or two. Can I see Logan now?"

"Follow me. We'll want to keep your cousin overnight, just to make sure he's in the clear. You can come pick him up tomorrow."

I went with the doctor into Logan's room and nearly passed out from relief when I saw him sitting on the bed, grinning from ear to ear.

"Copper Top! I was wondering if you abandoned me to my fate."

"As if I would," I said, walking to the side of his bed. "If I know you, you're probably already being a demanding patient."

The doctor cleared his throat from the doorway and I turned to look at him.

"You've got about ten minutes, and then we'll need to run a few more tests on Logan. If you get a headache, please make sure you come back in. I don't believe you have a concussion, but just in case."

I nodded and turned back to Logan, punching him lightly on the arm.

"Good to see you're alive and kicking. Oh, shoot!"

"What?" Logan asked, looking around with alarm.

"I should have called Kelsie."

I automatically reached for my pocket where I usually kept my phone and remembered Trish had taken it.

"It will be fine. I'm not sure I want her to see me like this, anyway," Logan said, gesturing to the hospital gown hanging loosely from his neck.

"Are you sure? I can borrow Zane's phone when we're done here."

"No, I'd rather wait and talk to her myself. I'll see if I can remember how to use one of these old-fangled devices," he said, pointing at the ancient phone on the table next to the bed.

"Logan, I am so sorry..."

He held up a hand and shook his head.

"Not a word. Not one regret. You did what you had to do, and you were right. One of them killed Sean."

"Yeah, and she almost killed you. I had no clue it was her. I feel terrible that I got you into that mess."

"Better me than you. That's all I gotta say. Finally, your hatred for sweet tea paid off."

I snorted as the door to Logan's room swung back open. A nurse poked her head in and smiled.

"Miss, I hate to ask you to leave, but we need to run some tests."

"No problem. Logan, be good," I said, rubbing his arm and looking into his eyes.

He snorted and gave me a crooked smile.

"When am I not good?"

"Um, like always? See you tomorrow."

"Sounds good. Oh, Brynn?"

"Hmmm?"

"Not one word to either of our mothers, you hear?"

I zipped my lips and walked back to the waiting room, briefly getting lost in the warren of hallways before finally finding my exit. Zane was in the same seat, holding Bernie like a baby. My beautiful cat was lightly batting his cheek, and I stopped to watch them for a second, emotion sitting in my throat like a lump. I didn't know how I'd gotten this lucky, but I wouldn't knock it.

There was nothing more I wanted to do than go home, but I knew there were a few things I needed to finish before I could sleep. I walked up behind Zane and put my hand on his shoulder.

"How's he doing?" Zane asked.

"He's his usual self. Which is a good thing."

Zane stood and handed Bernie over to me. I put my chin on the top of Bernie's head and held him closely as we walked outside.

"What now? I'm guessing you don't want to go straight home? You need to eat something, though."

"I know, but there are a few things I need to finish up. I can take Logan's truck and bring it back when I pick him up tomorrow."

Zane threw an arm over my shoulder and steered me towards his Jeep.

"Hop in. Let's head back to the cabin."

"There's a great burger place on the way back to my house from there. My treat."

"Sounds like a plan. But I'm buying."

We listened to music as Zane drove to the cabin. I looked out the window as the last light of the day fled and thought about how close I'd come to losing my best friend and cousin. Bernie sat up and stretched in my lap, ears twisting forward.

"Don't forget me when you get burgers later," Bernie said, licking his chops. "I'm starving."

I looked over at Zane and raised an eyebrow. He shook his head and gave me a sad smile.

"All I hear are meows, but I'm guessing he's got something to say."

"He wants a piece of my burger later."

Zane laughed and ruffled Bernie's head.

"Buddy, you can have a whole burger. If it wasn't for you, the woman I love wouldn't be sitting next to me."

My heart skipped a beat, and I glanced over at Zane. His handsome face flushed, and he looked uncharacteristically nervous. He swallowed hard and met my eyes.

"You don't have to say it back, Brynn. I know we just met a few weeks ago. It slipped out."

"No, I feel the same way," I said, watching as Zane's shoulders relaxed. "I wasn't sure how you felt."

He laughed like a kid and reached out for my hand. Bernie looked between us and shook his head.

"I hate to spoil the love fest between you two kids, but we need to talk about our next steps, Brynn."

"We're going to help Sean move on, right?"

"Of course, I wasn't talking about that. I mean about Ned."

I shrugged my shoulders and looked over at him.

"What's the difference? Won't it be just like I always do? I mean, I'm not even sure what I do, but somehow, when ghosts are ready to move on, they just kind of, well, move on."

Bernie licked his paw and shot me a look as he narrowed his eyes.

"You've got a lot to learn."

I glanced up and saw we were heading down the last road to the cabin.

"Well, we're about to the cabin," I said. "If you've got something to say, you better hurry."

Bernie rolled his eyes.

"Yeah, like I can condense that much teaching into a few minutes. Later, I mean. Now that we can communicate, we'll need to have daily lessons. And my food quality is going to need to improve."

"La-di-da, Mr. Picky," I said. "Do you think we'll be able to keep communicating after Ned moves on?"

He shrugged his little kitty shoulders and swiped over his face with a paw.

"We'll see."

I shook my head as Zane's Jeep rolled to a halt. I looked over at him and smiled.

"Ready for this?"

Zane nodded and opened his door.

"I'm always here for you, Brynn."

Bernie leapt out of the door once I opened it and hurried in front of me to the back of the cabin. I hustled after him, not wanting to lose sight of his black fur in the dark. Zane's longer legs meant he only needed to walk, and they both ended up beating me to the back deck.

I stood for a second, trying to catch my breath as I watched Bernie circle in the yard three times. He sat down and glanced over his shoulder at me.

"He's coming."

"Listen here, mister. We need to have a talk after all of this is said and done."

I felt a chill as the ghost of Sean Treadwell materialized in front of us. Zane rubbed at his arms and looked around.

"There you are. What happened? I feel different," Sean said, striding closer.

I quickly explained that we'd found his killer and broke the news that it was his girlfriend and how she did it. Sean blinked before nodding slowly. A sad look crept across his features.

"I knew something wasn't right between us, but I never thought she'd do something like that. I mean, she had a temper, but I can't imagine her doing all that."

He was quiet for a second and I reached for him, wishing there was a way I could comfort him.

"I'm sorry it was someone you were close to."

He met my eyes and nodded.

"I'm not sure we were ever that close, now that I look back at it. We were comfortable together but we were never crazy in love. You know, her dad is a hunter. She always went with him on his hunts and bagged a few of her own deer. She always bragged about how good she was at skinning and butchering. I guess she was right. What happens now?"

He looked dejected, and his shoulders were slumped. My heart twinged as I thought about the life he'd had ripped away, the plans he'd made that would never be accomplished.

"I'm so sorry, Sean. You deserved better. But now you can be at peace. Your mom is coming up to claim your body tomorrow. Is there anything you'd like me to tell her?"

"That I'm sorry, and I love her. I wish I could have been a better son."

"I'm sure you were an amazing son, Sean. You'll see each other again, I'm sure of it."

He looked over his shoulder as a light came through the trees. It swelled in size and the brightness of it made me squint.

"What's that?" Sean asked, looking into the light like he was mesmerized.

"It's time to go. Are you ready?"

He looked back at me before returning his eyes to the light. I watched as a smile spread over his face.

"I can see my grandpa," he said, voice full of wonder. "He's telling me to come. He's been waiting for me."

Tears filled my eyes as I nodded.

"I wish we could've met under better circumstances, Sean, but I'm glad I got to know you."

"I can just go into the light?"

I nodded, unable to speak as tears streamed down my face. I could hear beautiful music and a warm, peaceful feeling spread through my body. Sean looked at me one more time as he walked towards the light.

"Thank you for helping me," he said before turning back and walking forward.

The brightness obscured my vision before it faded completely, leaving me in the pitch black.

"Is it over?" Zane asked.

His voice was quiet in the night's stillness, and I walked over to him as my eyes adjusted.

"Sean's passed on. He saw his grandfather."

"Do you think that happens a lot?"

I nodded as I threaded my arm around his waist.

"Every time. Now, we need to figure out Ned," I said, looking for Bernie's eyes in the darkness.

"I'm over here. Ned's not responding," Bernie said as he stalked over to me, fur ruffled up.

"Do we need to wait?"

He walked past me and kept going, tail lashing back and forth.

"Up to you. I'm hungry. We can always come back."

I looked into the trees and frowned, not wanting to leave any loose ends. Ned had been wandering for over a hundred years. He'd mentioned being in another place before being pulled back here, but I didn't know where that place was, or how to send him back there. I shrugged and turned to move away.

As we walked around the house, a chilly wind blew through the trees, rustling their leaves. I stopped and peered into the blackness.

"Ned? Are you here?"

The wind whipped around and I heard a bang as one of the deck chairs blew over. Ned's familiar cackle echoed around me.

"Glad you're okay, girly. It's been nice having someone to conversate with."

"Ned, do you want to move on? I'm not sure how to do it, but I can try."

His form finally popped into sight right in front of me and I jumped. Zane tightened his arm around my back and looked around. Ned narrowed his eyes at Zane before giving a sharp nod.

"That other fella, is he okay?"

"He is. Thank you for helping us. Now, about moving on."

Ned gave another cackle and zipped around the clearing.

"I don't think so, girly. I'm having too much fun to go back to that other place just yet. Mebbe some other time."

"But Ned, you can't just stay here and keep scaring people. I know the descendant of the man who wronged you bought this place, but he's not the one who hurt you."

"You've got it all wrong," Ned said, shaking his finger at me. "I can do what I want."

"Ned, please. If you don't want to move on, at least promise me you won't keep scaring people."

His face took on a mulish expression and he spat on the ground.

"Mebbe. Mebbe not."

I stomped my foot and glared at him.

"Ned!"

"Aw, you're no fun. Fine, I won't scare the people. Much."

I figured that was as good as I was going to get. I turned to leave before stopping short.

"You said I had it all wrong. Do you want me to find out what really happened to you?"

Ned's face blanked, and he looked off into the distance before shrugging his misshapen shoulders.

"Might have you do that. We'll see."

He grinned again, spat the side right towards my feet and popped out of sight, laughing like a loon. I had a feeling we definitely hadn't seen the last of old Ned.

"Come on, Zane. Let's go get that burger. And find Bernie. Hopefully he didn't go too far."

A disgruntled meow came from my feet as I tripped over my cat.

"I'm right here, you know. Watch your step."

"Hey, I thought you left."

He turned in front of us and stalked back to the Jeep, tail held high. As we got in and started the long drive down the mountain, I told Zane what Ned said. He shook his head and laughed.

"I don't think I'll ever tire of you and your adventures."

His hand snaked across the seat and grabbed mine. I smiled as I looked out the window, admiring the lights of the cabins as we drove past. Bernie gave me a head bump, and I looked down at him.

"No ketchup on my burger, please. No bun either."

"Do you want cheese?" I asked, half teasing.

He cocked his head to the side before nodding.

"That would be acceptable."

I rolled my eyes and went back to gazing out the window. I wasn't sure what the future was going to hold, but I could finally communicate with my wonder cat. Logan was going to be okay, and Zane had professed his love for me. In my book, despite what happened today, I was going to score it as a win. I couldn't wait for our next adventure and I couldn't be happier that the people and cat I loved would be with me each step of the way.

NOW AVAILABLE! THE PREQUEL YOU'VE BEEN WAITING FOR!

The ABC's of Seeing Ghosts
A Soul Seeker Cozy Mystery Prequel Novella

High school is never easy. Neither is seeing ghosts.

Brynn Sullivan knows these two facts all too well. In this thrilling prequel to the Soul Seeker series, Brynn tries to balance going to school with helping the local Sheriff solve a murder.

Travel back in time to join Brynn, Logan, and Bernie as they they race to solve their first official case!

Grab your copy today!

BOOKS BY COURTNEY MCFARLIN

Escape from Reality Cozy Mystery Series

Escape from Danger

Escape from the Past

Escape from Hiding

A Razzy Cat Cozy Mystery Series

The Body in the Park

The Trouble at City Hall

The Crime at the Lake

The Thief in the Night

The Mess at the Banquet

The Girl Who Disappeared

Tails by the Fireplace

The Love That Was Lost

The Problem at the Picnic

The Chaos at the Campground

The Crisis at the Wedding

The Murder on the Mountain

The Reunion on the Farm

The Mishap at the Meeting - Summer 2023

A Soul Seeker Cozy Mystery

The Apparition in the Attic

The Banshee in the Bathroom

The Creature in the Cabin

HAVE YOU READ THE RAZZY CAT COZY MYSTERY SERIES?

The Body in the Park
A Razzy Cat Cozy Mystery

"I'm a cat lover and read many cat mysteries. Courtney McFarlin's Razzy Cat Cozy Mystery Series is my favorite."

She's found an unlikely consultant to help solve the crime. But this speaking pet might just prove purr-fect...

Hannah Murphy yearns for a real news story. But after a strange migraine results in an unexpected ability to talk to her cat, she must keep the kitty-communication skills a secret if she wants to advance from fluff pieces to covering felonies. And when she literally trips over a slain body, she's shocked her feline companion is the best partner to crack the case.

Convinced she's finally got her big break, Hannah quickly runs afoul of a handsome detective and his poor opinion of interfering reporters. And when she discovers the victim's penchant for embezzlement and fraud, she may need more than a furry friend and a cantankerous cop to avoid ending up in the obits.

Can Hannah catch a killer before her career and her life are dead and buried?

The Body in the Park is the delightful first book in the Razzy Cat cozy mystery series. If you like clever sleuths, light banter, and talking animals, then you'll love Courtney McFarlin's hilarious whodunit.

More reader comments: "The Razzy Cat series is a joy to read! I have read the first three, and just bought the fourth. These books are well written, engaging stories. I love the positive and supportive relationships depicted amongst the main characters and the cats. That is so refreshing to read. I look forward to more books in this series. I will also be reading some this author's other works. Well done, and keep writing!" - Ingrid

Buy *The Body in the Park* for the long arm of the paw today!

Keep reading for a sneak peek at Chapter One.

BONUS: CHAPTER ONE OF THE BODY IN THE PARK

Friday, June 19th

The hum of the newsroom refused to fade into the background as I worked to file my last story for the day. I'd been assigned a fluff piece, which I usually hated, but considering it was almost the weekend, I wouldn't complain too much. I was looking forward to two blissful days off and some quality time away from work.

I've been working at the paper here in Golden Hills, Colorado, for two years, ever since I graduated from the local college. I'm originally from a tiny town in South Dakota, and I love living so close to the mountains. I'd discovered a love of hiking while I was in college, and I couldn't imagine leaving to go back home to the family farm. There's nothing wrong with farming, we all gotta eat, but for me, I needed mountains and adventure.

I read through my story one more time, checking for errors, stopping to admire my byline. Hannah Murphy, that's me. Seeing my name in print never got old. I hit enter on my laptop, posting my story to my editor with plenty of time to spare on my deadline. I rummaged around under my desk, looking for my purse. With any luck, I'd be able to slip away a bit early and head home. I poked my head over my cubicle and looked over at the glass office where my editor, Tom Anderson, was banging away on his computer. I stifled a laugh. Tom was old school, from a time when the clerical girls typed everything on typewriters, and he resented being forced to use a computer.

I grabbed my things and headed down three cubicles to where my best friend, Ashley Wilson, worked. Ashley was my roommate in college, and we were both journalism majors. While she lived for the lifestyle pages, I was drawn to the hard news and wanted to make a name for myself as a reporter. I wasn't kidding myself. I knew it was a miracle our little newspaper had its doors open still. Most small newspapers had folded years ago, and it was tough for an independent outfit to keep the lights on. But I was hoping with some luck, perseverance, and hard work, I'd be able to move up the ranks to a serious news position.

I tapped on the wall of Ashley's cubicle and flopped into the chair across from her desk.

"Hey, Ash, you about done for the day?"

Her tongue was poking out from between her lips as she focused on her screen, ignoring me. I leaned over to see what was engrossing her and saw she was working on an image in Photoshop. Since we were such a small paper, most of us had to do our design work for our stories, which wasn't always fun.

I watched her as she worked, admiring her long brown hair that was impossibly straight and glossy. My hand went up to my unruly nest of blonde locks, and I gave a rueful smile. No matter how often I tried to straighten my hair, it never turned out as pretty as hers.

We were complete opposites. She was tall, statuesque, and dark, while I was short, thin, and fair. She enjoyed shopping and partying, while I was an outdoors kind of girl. It didn't matter, though. I'd never had a friend as close as her. She gave a little shout and hit save, turning to face me.

"Hey Hannah, sorry about that. The image didn't want to cooperate."

"No worries, been there, done that. What are your plans for tonight? Are you hanging out with Bill, or was it Will?"

"Will. He was also three guys ago. You gotta keep up, girl!"

"Sorry, are you hanging out with what's his face tonight?"

"I was unless you wanted to do something. We need a girl's night out."

"We do, but not tonight. I think I've got a migraine coming on. I'll just go home and hang out with my cat."

Ashley made a sad face and heaved a sigh.

"That's how it starts. You're in your twenties, and you spend a Friday night alone, with just a cat for company. Before I know it, you'll be my crazy cat lady friend who becomes a shut-in and only leaves to buy more cat food."

"Wow, that's a depressing and strangely detailed future look."

"I call them as I see them. I kid, Hannah. You should get out more, though," Ashley said, giving me a look.

"I know, I'm just not a peopley person. I enjoy being outside, not cramped in a loud bar with sweaty people being all, I don't know, sweaty. I like my cat. I like quiet."

"I need to find you a man. I think Will had a brother..."

"Thanks, but no thanks. I don't want to get set-up with a cast-off's brother. That would be even sadder than being home alone with my cat. Seriously though, have fun tonight. I expect a play-by-play tomorrow."

Her phone rang, cutting off our conversation. I waved as I grabbed my bag to leave. It looked like the coast was clear, so I headed towards the door, determined to make a break for it. I wasn't lying to Ashley, my head was pounding, and I wanted to get home and change into my jammies.

"Hannah! Wait!"

I groaned when I heard Tom's voice, turning in my tracks to head back to his office. I stopped in the doorway.

"Hi, Tom. How was my article? Does it need any edits?"

"It was fine. You self-edit well. That's not why I wanted to talk to you," Tom said, gesturing for me to come in and take a seat.

I plopped in the comfy chair across from his desk.

"What's up?"

The way Tom dressed was as old school as the way he typed. His button-down shirt was turned up at the cuffs, exposing a myriad of ink stains. He had a nice face, utterly at odds with his gruff voice. He scrubbed his bald head and leaned back in his chair. He looked at me closely for a beat.

"Hannah, you've been doing a great job lately. I know fluff pieces aren't what you want to do, and I appreciate you've been good about working on them. I can tell you put the effort in, even though you don't enjoy the subject."

"Thanks, Tom, that's nice of you to say."

"I'd like to try you out on a few tougher pieces. The next big story that breaks is yours."

"Are you serious? I'd love to try some harder news pieces!"

This was the most exciting thing to happen to me in months. I was finally going to sink my teeth into some meaty stories!

"That and whatever else you can dig up. I know you're young, but I think you deserve a shot."

"Thank you so much. I won't let you down."

"See that you don't."

With that, he waved me off and turned back to his computer, cursing under his breath as he started banging on the keys again.

I floated out of his office, almost forgetting my headache. I got to the parking lot and climbed into my ancient Chevy Blazer. I'd saved up my money back in high school, and it was old back then. It'd seen me through college, though, and with any luck, it would get me through until I could make enough money to replace it.

Traffic was picking up as I navigated my way back to my apartment. Golden Hills was growing fast, but I was lucky enough to find a place that backed right onto a huge green space. I had acres and acres of wilderness to explore via the trail that led to the Crimson Corral park. It wasn't cheap, but it was worth it to have an outdoor space and a killer view.

I trudged up to the top floor, feeling my headache get worse with every step. By the time I made it to my door, I was feeling odd. I walked in and immediately tripped over my cat, Razzy. I'd had her for two years, ever since I got my place. I scooped her up and cuddled her close, apologizing for tripping over her. She was a Ragdoll cat, and I had no idea how a beautiful, purebred cat like her had ended up in an animal shelter.

Her soft fur felt like a rabbit, and her little purrs made me smile. She was a quiet cat who rarely meowed. I put her down and walked to the kitchen, trying to decide what to make for supper. A quick check of the fridge revealed I needed to do some serious grocery shopping. As I stood in front of my cabinets, a wave of nausea and dizziness rushed through my body. I gripped the counter to keep from falling over.

Razzy meowed at me, cocking her head to the side. It was like she could tell something was wrong. I skipped dinner and walked back to my bedroom, holding my head. I changed into my favorite pair of fuzzy pajama pants and a tank top. Maybe if I just lay down for a few minutes, I'd feel better. I collapsed onto the bed, and Razzy jumped up next to me, snuggling close. Closing my eyes, I felt darkness rush towards me.

* * *

"Mama? Mama!"

A small voice pulled me from the darkness. I blinked open my eyes, trying to get my bearings. I felt grass underneath my feet. I looked around and realized I was in a park. My stomach felt hollow as I looked around, trying to figure out why I was outside. I glanced down and saw I was still wearing my fuzzy pants and smiled. This must be a dream. At least, in my dream, I didn't have my headache.

"Mama?"

There was that voice again. I looked through the gloom, trying to see if a child was wandering around. This was a strange dream for sure.

"Mama! There you are."

A small figure walked towards me and sat in front of me, looking up into my face. It took me a second to recognize my cat, Razzy, sitting there. Her whiskers bristled in the faint light from the moon.

"Say something, Mama. You're scaring me. Why are you outside?"

I felt my world rock as I realized Razzy was talking to me. Like, really talking. I laughed when I remembered I was dreaming. Geez, this was one crazy dream. I shrugged and went with it.

"Razzy, what are you doing in my dream?"

"Um, I'm pretty sure you're not dreaming. I followed you out of the apartment. You left the door open, which isn't safe, by the way. I tracked you here and kept calling you until I found you. Why didn't you answer me?"

Ok, this was weird. She was talking to me like she was a human, and I could understand everything she was saying. This had to be the winner for my strangest dream ever.

"You were calling for mama. I figured there was a little kid in my dream who was looking for their mother. I didn't know it was you."

"I always call you that. To me, you are my mama," Razzy said, her eyes rounding with concern. "This is weird, though. I always try to talk to you, but it's like you can't understand me. Why are you suddenly understanding what I say?"

"Must be the dream. I'm sure I'm going to wake up any second and find you cuddled up next to me."

"You're not dreaming, but whatever. Can we go home now? It's getting cold."

Razzy fluffed up her fur and turned to her left, looking at me expectantly. Her tail curled into a question mark as I stood there, staring at her. Well, maybe if I followed her, I'd wake up. I must have had something bad for lunch.

I shrugged and followed her.

"Lead on, MacDuff," I said, as I fell in behind her.

"It's actually 'Lay on, MacDuff,'" Razzy said with a sniff. "Humans, always misquoting things."

"Wait, you know Shakespeare?"

"I know way more than you might think."

I couldn't help but laugh. I had a talking cat who was also a literary critic in this dream. I needed to write this down when I woke up.

Razzy paused, her tail going stiff and then curling down behind her. Her hackles went up, and she sniffed the air.

"Stop, there's something up ahead."

"Are we going to meet a talking dog next? That would be pretty cool."

I moved past her, ready to get out of this dream and wake up back in my apartment. I took a few more steps and fell over something stretched across the sidewalk. As I felt around to see what I'd tripped over, my hand came in contact with something cold and squishy. With a little shriek, I scooted back. This dream had taken a disturbing turn.

I felt in the pocket of my pajama pants and grabbed my cell-phone. Switching on the flashlight app, I held it out in front of me, my hands shaking. I wasn't sure I wanted to see what it illuminated.

There, next to me on the ground, was the body of a man. I placed my fingers on his neck and felt nothing there. Jumping up, I screamed, convinced now was the perfect time for me to wake up. I looked over at Razzy. She walked closer, sat down, and shook her head.

"I told you, you're not dreaming. You should probably call the cops."

Realization flooded through me as I took stock of the situation. My feet were freezing on the cold concrete. I checked my arms and noticed I had goosebumps. I pinched myself and winced when I clearly felt it.

Razzy walked over to my feet and gently bit down on the top of my foot.

"Ouch! Why did you do that?" I asked, rubbing my foot.

"You didn't seem to believe me you're awake. You were pinching yourself, so I thought it would help if I pitched in too." She gave what I assumed to be the cat version of a shrug. "Call the cops."

173

I hesitated for a second before numbly obeying her suggestion and punching 9-1-1 in on my phone.

Get your copy now to read the rest!

A NOTE FROM COURTNEY

Thank you for taking the time to read this novel. If you enjoyed the book, please take a few minutes to leave a review. As an independent author, I appreciate the help!

If you'd like to be first in line to hear about new books as they are released, don't forget to sign up for my newsletter. Click here to sign up! https://bit.ly/2H8BSef

A LITTLE ABOUT ME

Courtney McFarlin currently lives in the Black Hills of South Dakota with her fiancé and their two cats.

Find out more about her books at:
   www.booksbycourtney.com

Follow Courtney on Social Media:

https://twitter.com/booksbycourtney

https://www.instagram.com/courtneymcfarlin/

https://www.facebook.com/booksbycourtneym

Made in the USA
Monee, IL
27 November 2024

71453015R00106